29 Breakout!

LEFT BEHIND
>THE KIDS<

Jerry B. Jenkins

Tim LaHaye

WITH CHRIS FABRY

TYNDALE KIDS

TYNDALE HOUSE PUBLISHERS, INC.
WHEATON, ILLINOIS

Visit Tyndale's exciting Web site at www.tyndale.com

Discover the latest Left Behind news at www.leftbehind.com

Left Behind is a registered trademark of Tyndale House Publishers, Inc.

Published in association with the literary agency of Alive Communications, Inc., 7680 Goddard Street, Suite 200, Colorado Springs, CO 80920.

Edited by Curtis H. C. Lundgren

ISBN 0-8423-5793-9, mass paper

Printed in the United States of America

08 07 06 05 04 03
8   7   6   5   4   3   2   1

To Greg, Diana, and Monte

TABLE OF CONTENTS

THE YOUNG TRIBULATION FORCE

Original members—Vicki Byrne, Judd Thompson, Lionel Washington

Other members—Mark, Conrad, Darrion, Janie, Charlie, Shelly, Melinda

OTHER BELIEVERS

Natalie Bishop—Morale Monitor in Des Plaines, Illinois

Jim Dekker—GC satellite operator helping the kids

Chang Wong—Chinese teenager working in New Babylon

Westin Jakes—pilot for singer Z-Van

Tsion Ben-Judah—Jewish scholar who writes about prophecy

Colin and Becky Dial—Wisconsin couple with an underground hideout

Bo and Ginny Shairton, Maggie Carlson, Manny Aguilara—escapees from GC jail

UNBELIEVERS

Nicolae Carpathia—leader of the Global Community

Leon Fortunato—Carpathia's right-hand man

Z-Van—lead singer for the popular group, The Four Horsemen

What's Gone On Before

VICKI Byrne and the rest of the Young Tribulation Force are living the adventure of a lifetime. With the help of Morale Monitor Natalie Bishop, Vicki and Darrion narrowly escape Global Community Peacekeepers in Des Plaines, Illinois, and reunite with friends in Wisconsin.

In spite of Lionel Washington's advice, Judd Thompson Jr. meets with a Chinese teenager in New Babylon. The boy, Chang Wong, turns out to be a believer, terrified because his father wants him to work for the Global Community.

Vicki and the others in Wisconsin send a 3-D computer program called The Cube to thousands and see great results. Together they conceive a plan to rescue other friends behind bars in Des Plaines.

Judd and Lionel get an urgent message from Chang and set a watch on his apartment building. Their plan is to hide Chang until they can secretly take him to Israel.

Natalie sees officials apply Carpathia's mark to prisoners. When a believer, Zeke Sr., is led into the application area, he bravely refuses to take the mark. Natalie secretly watches as the man prays for his enemies and loses his life.

Join the Young Tribulation Force as they enter the most dangerous era in history.

ONE

Bad News

VICKI and the others in the Dials' underground Wisconsin hideout gathered around the television. It was two in the afternoon, and the kids expected the worst about Zeke Sr. Vicki held the phone while Mark Eisman monitored e-mail, both hoping Natalie would find a way to contact them.

An earlier news report had said the first mark application had begun at a GC facility in Wheaton, formerly known as the DuPage County Jail. Other mark applications were scheduled that afternoon in various local jails and prisons.

The kids had rejoiced when Conrad called with the news of the escape of Ginny and Bo Shairton, Maggie Carlson, and a former gang member who was now a believer, Manny

Aguilara. All four were now in the home of Jim Dekker, a GC satellite operator from Illinois who had helped the kids.

Vicki prayed for Natalie. As far as Vicki knew, Global Community Peacekeepers hadn't discovered that the four former inmates were actually free.

Mark fiddled with the TV antenna to pull in the Chicago station.

Finally, a reporter in Wheaton, Illinois, broke into the newscast. "As we've reported, the mark applications began here a little after noon today. With the new technology, Peacekeepers wondered if there would be any glitches in the system. We're told that everything went fine until the last prisoner was brought into the application room and refused to take the mark.

"That set in motion a series of events that local Peacekeepers say was regrettable, but necessary."

The broadcast cut to a video feed of an interview with Deputy Commander Darryl Henderson. The man pursed his lips and shook his head. "We brought this prisoner from Des Plaines and gave him every chance to comply with the simple requirement of taking the mark of loyalty. When he refused, we had no alternative."

"Is it true you didn't expect to need the guillotine?" the reporter said.

"It's a loyalty enforcement facilitator," Henderson corrected. "No, we assumed that our prison population would all take the mark. Everyone did except for this one man."

The scene switched to the reporter looking at his notes. "That one man is identified as fifty-four-year-old Gustaf Zuckermandel, formerly of Des Plaines. He had been charged with black market trafficking of fuel oil, but sources inside this facility tell me he was a follower of the dissident Tsion Ben-Judah. Officials say they hope this execution will serve as a warning to other Judah-ite followers that this kind of defiance of the Global Community will not be tolerated."

Mark turned off the television and the kids sat in silence. Vicki thought of Zeke Jr. and wondered if he knew about his father's death. There was no denying the clear facts. They had now entered a bloody season when believers in Christ would be hunted and if caught, executed. Vicki shuddered. If she and Darrion had been caught in Des Plaines, they would have been forced to choose Carpathia's mark or the blade. Would she have chosen to die for what she believed? Would she have to make that choice in the future?

The phone rang and Vicki answered it. Conrad wanted to know if the kids had heard about Zeke, and Vicki said they had.

"We're staying at Jim Dekker's farmhouse until things settle," Conrad said. "He wants us to take supplies with us when we go."

"What do you mean?"

"GC uniforms, ID cards—you name it, he's got it."

Mark talked with Conrad after Vicki was through, and then the kids met to discuss their next move.

"We can't slow down now," Melinda said. "We have to tell as many people as we can before they take the mark."

"Pretty soon there won't be anyone left who's undecided," Janie said. "Then we'll just have to try and survive."

"What's important right now is getting the message to as many unbelievers as possible," Darrion said, "and our best tool is The Cube. It's high-tech and gets people's attention. We should send the file and look for any other ways to get the message out."

The phone rang again and Vicki jumped. Mark answered and handed it to her. "It's Natalie."

Lionel Washington hid in some bushes near the Global Community apartment building where Chang Wong and his parents stayed. Judd had given him Chang's description, but Lionel was nervous. What if someone who looked like Chang came out of the building? Lionel was glad Judd would be back early in the morning.

Nights in New Babylon felt eerie to Lionel. The blistering heat of the day gave way to cool air once the sun went down. A breeze blew through the bushes, and Lionel hunkered down in his hiding place.

Lionel had witnessed incredible things in the past few weeks. He had seen the deaths of the beloved prophets, Eli and Moishe, and a few days later had watched them ascend into heaven. That had been one of the high points of their trip to Israel. But soon after came Carpathia's murder and his eventual rise from the dead. Every time Lionel thought about it, he recalled the lightning of Leon Fortunato and the bodies of innocent victims lying in the palace courtyard.

The door opened at the front of the apartment building, and a guard strolled out front, lighting a cigarette. He walked to within a few feet of Lionel's hiding place and flicked cigarette ashes into the bushes.

Thanks for using our world as your ashtray, Lionel thought, recalling the words of his father. Lionel smiled as he remembered driving in the car with his dad. A motorist would pass, flicking ashes or a spent cigarette to the pavement, and Lionel's dad would shake his head. Once Lionel's father had stepped out of the car at a stoplight, picked up a smoldering butt off the ground, and handed it to the driver through the open window.

"I think you dropped this," Lionel's father had said, then returned to the car before the light changed. He buckled up and stifled a smile. "Don't tell this to your mother."

Lionel missed his dad more than he wanted to admit. They had missed so many things. With each birthday or holiday, Lionel ached for some kind of celebration, a cake, or some presents. But the truth was, the kids didn't have time for things like that. Life was a constant struggle.

At moments like these, when Lionel was alone, he thought about his family, his mother's smile, his father's strength. Most of the kids he knew from school had parents who were divorced. His mom and dad had stayed together through some rough times and Lionel was glad.

The guard flicked the spent cigarette into the bush where Lionel was hiding and walked away. The glowing ashes faded and finally went out. It was just like the world, Lionel thought, dying and almost dead.

He drew his knees to his chest, wrapped himself in the light jacket he was wearing, and leaned back. The night chill and lack of activity inside the building made his eyelids droop.

When he fell asleep, he was thinking of his father.

Vicki tried to comfort Natalie, but the girl was nearly hysterical. When she finally calmed down, Vicki discovered that Natalie was at her apartment, having told her boss she wasn't feeling well.

Natalie told Vicki about her experience at the old DuPage County Jail. She had heard Zeke protest about the mark of loyalty. She had followed the man and had watched from an observation room when the Global Community ended Zeke's life.

"You actually saw the beheading?"

"I couldn't watch, but I heard the blade come down. One guy in the room raised his fist and said Zeke got what he had coming to him. How can people be that cruel?"

"I don't know. Are you all right now?"

Natalie sighed. "I just feel so alone. The GC are all saying everything went exactly as planned, but I know the truth. All those prisoners who took the mark can *never* become believers now, and they killed the only one who had the sense to not take it."

"Does Henderson suspect anything about the four who escaped?"

"Not that I can tell. He's been too busy with the mark applications to notice much, but I heard they're still looking for you."

"We're safe. Any idea how long before employees get the mark?"

"Henderson's sending a report to other facilities throughout the country. Jails and reeducation facilities will apply the mark for the next couple of days. Then employees are eligible. We have two weeks to comply after it's up and running."

"Then you have to come here."

"Believe me, I can't stop thinking about it. But I'm so mad. After what I saw Zeke go through, why does God let this happen?"

"I understand how you feel. I felt the same thing when my friend Ryan died."

"Why couldn't somebody have told us about God before all this happened?"

"They tried, at least they did with me," Vicki said. "I wouldn't listen."

"So we just have to sit back and watch all of these good people get their heads chopped off? Is that what God wants?"

Natalie broke down and sobbed. Vicki listened and tried to calm her. Suddenly, Natalie put her hand over the phone and said, "Hi, Claudia. Yeah, you should have been there." When Natalie uncovered the phone, she whispered, "My roommate's here. I'll call you later and we can talk."

Vicki gathered the other kids to pray for Natalie. She knew the girl's time was running out.

Judd Thompson Jr. crept through the darkened streets of New Babylon. A few cabs sat parked by the street, drivers slouched and snoring in their seats. A strip of yellow and white shone on the horizon as Judd looked at his watch. 6:30 A.M. *I should have relieved Lionel an hour ago!*

Judd located the shrubs and found Lionel sleeping. Lionel awoke with a start, and Judd put a hand over his mouth. "How long have you been asleep?"

Lionel rubbed his neck and yawned. "I don't know. It was so cold and I just couldn't keep my eyes open."

"I can't blame you. I'm late myself."

"No word from Chang?"

"Nothing," Judd said. "But Z-Van came in late last night jazzed up."

"About his recording?"

Judd shook his head. "He was crowing about getting to take the mark today. They're taking pictures for the album cover, and he wants to make sure he has Carpathia's mark. And get this. He's supposed to have a picture taken with Carpathia."

"If they're letting Z-Van take the mark, that means—"

Judd pointed toward the front door of the apartment building. A man with a briefcase walked inside. The guard checked the man's credentials and waved him through.

"I saw that guy at Carpathia's funeral," Judd said. "Moon, I think. He's in Carpathia's inner circle."

"Maybe he lives there."

Judd shook his head. "I wish we had some binoculars."

Lionel reached inside his jacket pocket and pulled out a tiny telescope. "Westin gave it to me before we left last night. Works pretty well."

Judd set the digital meter for the distance and zoomed in on the scene. The scope was so powerful he could see the badge of the guard at the front door. He focused on the elevators and saw one had stopped on the fourth floor.

"That's Chang's floor," Judd said.

Vicki had trouble falling asleep, a thousand thoughts swirling through her mind. It had been some time since they had heard from Judd and Lionel, and she was worried they might be in trouble. And she thought of Zeke. She couldn't shake the image of the razor-sharp blade falling.

She had just gotten to sleep when Shelly shook her. "You need to come see something."

Vicki dressed quickly and walked into the meeting area of the underground hideout. Mark had the kids' Web site up on the large screen at the front of the room.

"You'll want to sit down for this," Shelly said.

"What's wrong?"

Mark showed Vicki the number of messages from people who had received The Cube. Many of them had prayed to become believers because of the 3-D tool. Mark scrolled to the bottom and pulled up a message whose subject line simply said *Help!*

*Vicki or anyone else working with the
Young Tribulation Force,*

*I'm typing this fast, so if I make mistakes
forgive me. I'm Kelly Bradshaw from Iowa.
You came to our meeting place at an abandoned college. I hope you remember us.*

"I remember Kelly," Vicki said. "She was
the first to meet us when we got there."

*We've had incredible growth since you
came and taught us. Word spread and
people came from all over to meet other
believers and read the notes we'd taken.
Then, when you sent The Cube, we almost
doubled in size. People brought friends who
hadn't seen it to the locker room under the
gym where we meet.*

*Someone must have tipped off the Global
Community because several Peacekeepers
burst into one of our smaller meetings
tonight and arrested everyone. I was on my
way back to our farm when I heard them
coming, but there was nothing I could do.
They raided the house where some of us
live, too, and took computers and supplies.
We had printed copies of Buck Williams's
The Truth to hand out to people who were
interested.*

We had a computer hidden in a secluded

room. That's where I am now, but I'm so afraid for my friends. Can you help? I'm hearing they are forcing prisoners to take the mark, so we don't have much time. Please, if there's anything you can do, let me know quickly.

"Have you written her back?" Vicki said.

Mark nodded. "I told her we'd be back to her within the hour. What do we want to say?"

Vicki looked around the room. "I say these are our brothers and sisters. We have to try."

Mark smiled. "That's what I thought you'd say."

TWO

Chang's Surprise

Judd kept the scope focused on the elevators and tried to remember as much as he could about the man named Moon. Judd hoped that the elevator stopping on Chang's floor was just a coincidence.

"Is Moon head of security?" Lionel said.

Judd racked his brain but couldn't recall anything more than Moon's face on the official GC Web site. A few minutes passed and Judd felt better. "I was probably overreacting."

Lionel took the scope and looked toward the tinted windows that lined the side of the building. He focused on the lobby and handed the scope back to Judd. "Elevator's coming down."

Judd quickly focused on the elevator doors and saw Mr. Wong and the GC official helping someone out. They headed toward the front door and Judd strained to see. The third person wore khakis, a light jacket, and had a red baseball cap pulled low over his eyes. The three turned before they reached the front door and headed down a corridor. "That has to be Chang."

Judd and Lionel darted out of their hiding place and walked to the side of the building to get a better look.

"Westin said there are tunnels that connect these buildings," Lionel said. "No telling where they're going."

Judd studied the structures behind the apartment complex. "It could be in any of those, and they're all guarded."

The two ran back to the hotel and squeezed into a phone booth. Judd dialed the Wongs' apartment, and Mrs. Wong answered on the first ring. She sounded upset.

"Mrs. Wong, where's Chang?"

The woman sniffed. "Who is this?"

"I'm Chang's friend. I know your husband didn't want me to call, but I'm concerned about—"

"They take him away just now. He so scared, they give him something to make him calm."

"They drugged him? Why?"

"He afraid of needle. They only try to make him calm."

"What needle? Where did they take him?"

"I'm not sure which building. They have meeting later, after Chang get mark."

Judd felt the air go out of the phone booth. Lionel asked what was wrong, but Judd couldn't speak. If they tried to give Chang Carpathia's mark, he wouldn't accept it. They would find out he was a believer in Christ and use the guillotine.

"You still there?" Mrs. Wong said.

"Yes," Judd choked.

"Everything will be all right. I talk with Chang. He take mark and everything be okay."

Judd placed the phone on the cradle and muttered, "No, it won't be okay." He told Lionel what Mrs. Wong had said.

Lionel slammed his fist against a wall, and several guests in the hotel glared at him. He slumped over. "I guess we're too late."

Judd and Lionel went up to Z-Van's penthouse suite and found Westin Jakes, Z-Van's pilot. The man grimaced when he heard about Chang. "We can't give up. Maybe they haven't given him the mark yet."

"There's nothing we can do," Lionel said.

"Do you know anyone else inside the GC?"

Judd shook his head. "Wait. I met this Peacekeeper a few days ago and promised to get Z-Van's autograph. Maybe he could help us."

Judd dug a card out of his pocket and read the name Roy Donaldson. "He told me he was originally from Florida."

Westin took the name and grabbed a pen and some paper from a nearby desk. "Call him and ask him to meet you in front of the apartments. I'll see if Z-Van's in good enough shape to scribble his name."

Vicki immediately called Jim Dekker's house in Illinois and explained the Iowa situation to Conrad. After she had talked with Jim, the man agreed to supply uniforms and IDs. Colin Dial would continue to pose as Commander Blakely, and they would travel in the van that already bore the GC insignia.

"How fast can you guys get here?" Conrad said.

"We're on our way," Vicki said.

Judd and Lionel found Peacekeeper Roy Donaldson pacing in front of the GC apartment building. Lionel shook hands with him and said, "So you're a big Z-Van fan?"

Roy smiled. "You bet. I liked him even

before he started singing about the potentate, but I can't wait for his new album."

Judd pulled a slip of paper from his pocket and gave it to Roy. He unfolded it carefully, like it was a priceless artifact. "'To Roy,'" he read aloud. "'He is risen.'"

At the bottom of the page was Z-Van's scrawled signature. Judd wanted to tell Roy that the singer's real name was Myron and that he was a jerk, but Judd didn't have the heart or the time.

"How about a little favor?" Judd said.

"Name it."

"Where are they giving employees the mark?"

Roy pointed to a building behind the apartments. "Building D. Man, I can't wait to get mine. I'm scheduled for this afternoon, but they may not be able to get to me until tomorrow."

"Could you take us there?"

Roy studied the autograph again. "After this, I'll do anything for you guys. Come on."

As they walked, Judd asked if Roy had heard anything about a potential employee named Chang Wong.

Roy stopped. "Don't tell me you know him too."

Judd smiled. "Yeah, he's a friend of mine."

Roy shook his head. "Kid's just a teenager like us and he's already a celebrity. A friend of mine works in the department looking at him. I hear this Wong kid's a genius with computers."

"He's a pretty nice guy too," Judd said.

"He seemed kind of uppity to me."

"You've met him?"

"I just saw him earlier." Roy pointed out the entrance and a line of employees snaking through the front door. People on the sidewalk craned their necks to see how much farther until they were inside.

"Wait," Judd said, grabbing Roy's arm. "You saw Chang?"

"Yeah, I got a look at him walking with Walter Moon and some other guy heading upstairs. I know it sounds like sour grapes and all, and I understand why new hires are getting the mark first, but—"

"Chang already has the mark?"

Roy rolled his eyes. "Yeah, I saw it, even with that stupid baseball cap he was wearing. He got a little *30* next to his eyebrows, nothing like what I'm going to have."

"Are you sure it was him?" Lionel said.

Roy cocked his head. "You don't see too many Asian kids around here who have the mark before other employees, do you? Of course I'm sure."

Judd looked at Lionel and cringed.

"You want me to see if I can get you guys in D?"

"Not now," Judd said.

"Well, don't think you're going to get a mark before us employees. Have you decided which one you're getting?"

Judd shook his head and glanced at the employees waiting to seal their fates. They were like sheep being led to the slaughter, and they didn't even know it.

Judd thanked Roy, and the Peacekeeper walked away clutching Z-Van's autograph.

Lionel sat down hard on a bench. "I don't get it. Tsion said God would give believers the strength they needed to resist taking the mark."

"Maybe it's not real," Judd said. "Maybe Chang came up with a fake that convinced everybody."

"Maybe. But there's another possibility."

"What's that?"

"Maybe Chang is fake himself."

Vicki rode with Mark and Shelly toward the farmhouse in McHenry, Illinois. Though the others had put up a fight, everyone finally agreed that it was best for a smaller group to help the teens in Iowa. Vicki felt tired but knew she wouldn't sleep until they were in the van and headed west.

Vicki wept when she saw Bo and Ginny Shairton and Maggie Carlson. They hugged and shared stories. Maggie said she was worried about Natalie and wished the girl would leave the Des Plaines jail.

Vicki greeted Jim Dekker, the satellite operator who had helped her escape the GC chase, then shook hands with Manny Aguilara, the prisoner who had become a believer after talking with Zeke. She handed Colin Dial a letter from his wife.

Mark shook hands with Jim Dekker. "It's a pleasure meeting the guy who came up with The Cube."

Dekker smiled and thanked him.

"I hate to break up this admiration society meeting," Conrad said, "but we don't have much time." He took the others to the basement and fitted them with Morale Monitor uniforms while Jim took their photos and created new ID cards.

Jim provided walkie-talkies and gave Mark a cell phone. "Make sure you keep in contact with us. Natalie will do what she can on her end, but we have to work together."

The night was still and a wind had come up in the east as the kids loaded supplies and

equipment into the van. Everyone gathered
and joined hands. One by one they prayed
for safety for the rescue group and the believers in Iowa. Manny, who had been part of
the group only a short time, prayed, "God,
we trust you to help your children. Show
them where to go and what to do."

Mark got behind the wheel for the first leg of
the trip as Colin and Conrad explained the
plan.

"How do we know they haven't already
applied the mark?" Vicki said.

Colin shook his head. "Jim and Natalie
diverted a shipment of injector machines.
They were going to do the same thing to the
guillotines, but for some reason shipments
have been delayed in North Carolina,
Florida, Iowa, and Tennessee. We don't have
any idea why."

Vicki put her head on the seat and pulled a
Morale Monitor jacket over her arms. The
uniform felt stiff, and Vicki wondered about
the girl who had worn it. Was she dead? Did
the horsemen get her or perhaps the earthquake?

As the conversation continued in the front,
Vicki felt sleep come over her. She thought of
the kids in Iowa. They had to be terrified.
And how long would it take the GC to realize

that Commander Blakely was really Colin Dial, a Judah-ite in disguise?

Vicki prayed for the believers behind bars and asked God to help them. She also remembered Natalie and the shock she had gone through witnessing Zeke's death. When Vicki had prayed for all the names and faces she could think of, she thought of Judd. She always kept him last. Sometimes she fell asleep praying for him and thinking of what he might be doing. She wondered if he missed her as much as she missed him. There were nights when she would dream of Judd standing up to Carpathia or telling strangers about God. Once she dreamed about his speech in front of Leon Fortunato at Nicolae High, and she woke up in a cold sweat.

Now, as she drifted in and out of sleep with the droning of the van's engine, she prayed that God would protect Judd from the evil forces loose in New Babylon and the rest of the world. She knew from reading Tsion Ben-Judah's letters that they weren't just fighting against the Global Community.

Tsion had often quoted a verse from Ephesians, chapter 6 which said, "For we are not fighting against people made of flesh and blood, but against the evil rulers and authorities of the unseen world, against those mighty powers of darkness who rule this world, and against wicked spirits in the heavenly realms."

When Vicki thought of doing battle with those wicked spirits, another verse from Ephesians came to mind. "Put on all of God's armor so that you will be able to stand firm against all strategies and tricks of the Devil." Carpathia's mark was a deadly trick of the devil himself.

Mark tuned the radio to a news station and kept it low. The reporter repeated several stories about mark application sites in the United North American States being behind in their application of the mark on prisoners.

The cell phone rang and Mark picked up. After a few moments he hung up and slowed the van.

"What's going on?" Vicki said.

"That was Jim Dekker. He's changing our route."

"Is something wrong?"

Mark shrugged. "Maybe it's a roadblock."

Vicki laid back and prayed again that God would protect them until they could help their friends in Iowa.

THREE

Rendezvous

VICKI wanted to ask Jim Dekker why they were turning, but Mark shook his head. "Dekker said we'd understand when we got there."

"But the kids in Iowa are going to die if we don't get there in time!"

"I understand. Jim does too. But he still told us to take a different road."

Headlights flashed on downed trees and an open field. Crude crosses rose from mounds of earth. Vicki guessed it was a graveyard filled with bodies of people killed by the earthquake, the horsemen, or some other disaster.

Mark had planned on taking back roads, concerned that a GC squad car might stop them, but Jim Dekker's call had taken them onto an interstate. They passed an 18-wheeler and a few cars but saw no GC.

They had been driving on the interstate a half hour when they came to the mile marker Dekker had given. Mark pulled into the entrance of an abandoned weigh station and stopped.

"What now?" Vicki said.

Mark took out the cell phone. "I don't like this any more than you. I'm calling Dekker."

Mark had the phone opened and was dialing when Vicki noticed headlights behind them. Colin Dial told everyone to get down.

"He led us into a trap," Conrad said.

"Just stay calm," Colin said.

Air brakes whooshed behind them. Mark stayed behind the wheel, ready to pull away. Colin got out of the van and walked back toward the truck.

"Can you see who it is?" Shelly whispered to Vicki.

Vicki crawled to the rear of the van and peeked over the equipment and uniforms stacked on the backseat. She shielded her eyes but couldn't see anything because of the glare. "I think it's the truck we passed a few miles back."

Colin's footsteps crunched in the gravel by the road. He wore his commander's uniform, and Vicki thought he played the part well. He walked confidently toward the truck, shielding his eyes, and yelled, "Cut your lights!"

A man yelled something to him, and Colin approached the driver.

"I don't like this," Shelly said.

Colin trotted up to Mark's window and told him to move farther into the weigh station. Colin stood on the running board and stuck his head in Mark's window. "Vicki, I need you out here."

Judd and Lionel found a film crew and several security personnel clogging the hallway in front of Z-Van's hotel suite. When they finally made it to the door, a man held up a hand. "Move along. This is a closed set."

Judd scowled. "We're staying here."

"Right." The man spoke into a walkie-talkie and two burly men approached.

"Westin, are you in there?" Lionel yelled.

The man at the door clamped a hand over Lionel's mouth. "You want to make this easy or hard?"

Lionel struggled free, but the two men were on him. "Escort these gentlemen outside," the man at the door said.

"Hold it," Westin said, pushing his way through the crowd. "Those guys are with me."

Judd and Lionel shook free of the men and

stepped over cords and cables as they entered the room. Bright lights were set up near the piano, and a man with a handheld light meter moved around the room.

"What's going on?" Lionel said.

"Ever heard of Lars Rahlmost?" Westin said.

Judd nodded. "I've seen a couple of his movies."

Westin pointed to the corner where a blond-haired man in a leather jacket stood stroking a stubbly beard. His hair was pulled back in a ponytail that swished as he talked. Z-Van was next to him, smiling and laughing. "That's him. He's doing a documentary about Nicolae called *From Death to Life.* They're interviewing Z-Van and are going to film some of his appearances in Israel."

Judd took Westin into the next room and explained what they had seen and heard about Chang.

Westin sat on the bed. "I'm new to this. You've been telling me you can't take this mark and still be a believer. What gives?"

"I don't know," Judd said. "Maybe we'll clear the whole thing up when we talk to Chang."

"You think that's smart?" Lionel said. "He could be a plant by the GC."

"He has the mark of the believer. There has to be an explanation."

"Set up a meeting," Westin said. "I'll still get him out of here if he wants help."

Judd phoned Chang's number but there was no answer. He sent an e-mail asking Chang to get in touch as soon as possible.

Vicki climbed out of the van, her heart beating like a locomotive, and followed Colin. She noticed the truck had official GC insignias on its side and on the front license plate.

"What's going on?" Vicki said.

"You'll see," Colin said, leading her to the front of the truck.

The driver's door opened wide and a brawny man stepped out, his back to Vicki. He shook Colin's hand and patted him on the shoulder. When he turned, Vicki's mouth dropped open and her knees felt like they were going to buckle. "Pete!"

"Surprised to see me?" Pete Davidson said, hugging Vicki tightly.

"I haven't seen you since before our trip west!" Vicki said.

"I read about that on the Web site. You did pretty well for yourself, young lady."

Vicki explained to Colin how Judd had become friends with Pete after the wrath of the Lamb earthquake.

"I've been driving for Chloe's Trib Force co-op the last few months."

"How did you—?"

"I'll tell you all about it in the truck," Pete said. "Hop in."

Shelly joined Pete and Vicki as they got back on the road. Pete said he had e-mailed the kids and was going to stop at the schoolhouse, but Darrion had called his satellite phone and told him about the situation in Iowa. They had gotten the van and truck together using Jim Dekker's satellite connection.

Vicki wanted to hear the latest from Pete, but she guessed Darrion hadn't told him about Zeke Sr. Since Pete had known the man, he nearly drove off the road when he learned Zeke was dead. He got the rig back under control and drove in silence for a few minutes. The big man's chin quivered when he finally spoke. "I called him Gus just to get on his nerves. His first name was Gustaf, you know. If there was any better man on the face of the earth, I never met him. He and his son took me in and never charged me a Nick for any fuel or supplies."

As the miles rolled on, Pete told stories about Zeke and how generous he was. "You'd never know it by looking at him, but God made him real tender towards people. First time I met him I told my story of looking for my girlfriend after the earthquake. He listened for the longest time, then put his head down. I thought he had fallen asleep, but he was crying. He'd never met her, and he was sobbing like she was his own daughter."

After a few more stories, Vicki asked what Pete was hauling in the truck. He smiled and said, "Firewood."

"Who would need firewood this time of year?"

"The GC. You see, they don't call it firewood, but I do."

"What do they call it?"

"They call it loyalty silly taters or something like that."

Shelly gasped. "You mean guillotines?"

Pete nodded. "That and some of the injector thingies. There are trailers full of these head choppers all over the country, but somehow they keep getting destroyed by the Judah-ites. It's the weirdest thing."

Vicki shook her head. "I should have known when I heard about the missing guillotines that it was something like this."

"Problem is, they're easy to make. The ones we destroy get replaced by local companies in a few days. We've slowed the GC down a little, but not much."

"Won't the GC know you're destroying them?" Shelly said.

"Sometimes we change the shipping records so me and my buddies aren't even on the list. Other times, like this one, I borrow the trailer from an official GC driver."

"You mean steal it?"

"I guess you could call it that. I know some people might think it's wrong, but I figure the only reason these contraptions exist is to kill believers. If I can do something to stop it, I will."

"What happened to you after you left the schoolhouse and went back east?" Shelly said.

"I actually headed south for several runs to believers down there. Oh, your friend Carl Meninger says to say hello. He's still hiding from the GC in South Carolina with the people on that island."

"You mean Luke and Tom?" Vicki said.

Pete nodded. "The GC got pretty close to them while they were hunting for Carl, but they've got a good hiding place. And more and more people are becoming believers down there."

"How did you get official GC stickers for your truck?" Shelly said.

"Zeke Jr. arranged that a while ago. I'm on their official roster of freelance truckers available for 'sensitive loads' as they call it. I've hauled everything from uniforms to computers to those guillotines back there."

Pete took Vicki's walkie-talkie and radioed the van to take the next exit. They drove a few miles into the countryside to a long, metal building. Pete flashed his lights twice, a door creeped open, and Pete drove in.

A wrinkled little man wearing a green hat with a deer on the front helped Pete unhook his trailer and put on a new one. They loaded the injector devices into the new trailer and were back on the road in a few minutes.

"What will that guy do with the guillotines?" Vicki said when they reached the interstate.

"He and a couple of friends will unload them, pull them apart, and burn the wood. They'll keep the metal until they can figure out what to do with it."

Pete asked the latest about the kids, and Vicki detailed the GC chase and the hideout in Wisconsin. Pete was excited to hear about The Cube and asked about Judd.

"He and Lionel were in Israel for a long time, but now—"

"No, what about *Judd and you?*"

Shelly rolled her eyes. "She doesn't think anybody knows."

Pete laughed. "Doesn't take a rocket scientist to see you two were meant for each other."

Vicki blushed. "This isn't anybody's business."

Pete playfully socked her shoulder. "When it's my sister, it's my business, you get me? You can deny it all you want, but just the way you're reacting now tells me a lot."

Vicki smiled. "Can we change the subject?"

While Judd waited for a return message from Chang, Lionel stood in the doorway to the bedroom and watched Z-Van's interview. Lars, the filmmaker, sat with his back to the camera and asked Z-Van about his music, his past, and what attracted him to Carpathia.

"My music was going well, and I suppose everything would have kept going just as it had, but finding something to sing about, to write about, that has so much meaning makes me understand what my life is all about."

"Explain," Lars said.

"Well, making money is wonderful, selling lots of recordings, and having fans think you're a god is fantastic, but it's not until you find what your life focus is about that you really understand the meaning of art. The best paintings, the best music, even the best films, don't really come from you, they come from observing something *bigger* than you. When I first heard His Excellency, his speeches blew me away. He has a grasp of every detail of life. He knows how to point people toward a goal, which is peace, and take them there."

Z-Van talked about Nicolae's resurrection and what it was like to actually see it happen. When the interview was over, Lars turned to his staff and looked at his watch. "We have about two hours to get the equipment to the next site. Let's make it happen."

Lionel turned to Westin. "What's the next site?"

"Building D. Z-Van's going to be the first civilian to take Carpathia's mark."

FOUR

Z-Van's Mark

LIONEL and Westin followed Z-Van and the camera crew to Building D. Lionel offered to help move some of the heavy road cases filled with equipment, but the workers wouldn't let him.

It was a festive atmosphere inside with people stepping out of offices or lingering by watercoolers to get a glimpse of one of the most famous musicians in the world. People whispered and pointed when they saw Z-Van, and a few recognized the film director as well. When someone held out a pen and a piece of paper for an autograph, one of Z-Van's bodyguards pushed the person away and Z-Van waved. "Sorry."

As the camera crew set up, Z-Van and Lars ducked into a private office. A few minutes later, a uniformed Peacekeeper rushed into the room, followed by a full detail of Peacekeepers that stood guard by each entrance.

Lionel recognized Roy Donaldson, the Peacekeeper Judd had met earlier, and walked up to him. "Looks like you'll get to see Z-Van in person."

Donaldson smiled. "Better than that. I get two for one."

"What do you mean?"

"The potentate is on his way. He's going to watch Z-Van take the mark."

Vicki and Shelly talked with Pete as the truck rolled across the Illinois border. Vicki explained how they had met the Iowa group at a college about fifty miles from Des Moines. Though the campus was in ruins, the kids had organized a group to hear Vicki explain the message.

"Did many people believe?" Pete said.

Vicki nodded. "And as we moved west, it seemed like the crowds got bigger. People were desperate to hear the truth."

"I wish I had had the same success. I went south to tell some friends what happened, thinking they'd want to hear what I had to say, but most of them were either caught up with Carpathia or they just wanted to be left alone."

"I don't understand that," Shelly said. "We have something that will give them meaning, purpose, and life that won't end."

"I guess that's how people felt about me before the vanishings," Pete said. "They tried to tell me about God, and I labeled them religious nuts."

Shelly frowned. "I hadn't thought about it that way. I did the same thing."

Colin radioed from the van ahead that Natalie had traced the captured kids to a GC reeducation facility on the outskirts of Des Moines. Pete pulled over and everyone got in the van.

Colin outlined the plan and everyone received their assignments. Pete would deliver the injector machines after dark that evening, while the others cut a hole in the fence outside the camp. Jim Dekker would put an order in from the fictitious Commander Blakely that all suspected Judah-ites be separated and left outside overnight. That would give the kids a chance to get their friends' attention and free them. "Plus we don't have to set foot inside the camp," Colin said.

"Any idea when they'll start the mark applications?" Conrad said.

"They can't do a thing as long as I have the goods in the back of my truck," Pete said.

"Unless they get another shipment from somewhere," Colin said, "they won't be able to start until tomorrow. That should leave us enough time to get everyone out."

"How many believers are we talking about?" Pete said.

"The official word is that thirteen Judahites were taken into custody," Colin said.

"We should prepare for a few more in case these kids convinced some on the inside of the truth," Pete said. "I can handle them in my truck once I deliver my load."

"Why are you destroying the guillotines but delivering the injectors?" Shelly said.

"I have to deliver *something*," Pete said. "I figure the chip injectors are bad for the people who take it, but it doesn't kill any believers. Plus it gets me inside enemy lines."

The phone rang and Colin walked outside to talk with Jim Dekker. When he came back, he had a grave look. "Jim says that site now has a guillotine. They're just waiting on the chip injectors. We'll have to go in earlier than we thought, and maybe during daylight."

"How will we get them out?" Shelly said.

Colin sighed. "We need a decoy."

Judd saw nothing from Chang throughout the morning. He logged on to the kids' Web site and read the mountain of e-mails responding to The Cube. Many reported family members and friends finally realizing the truth after seeing it.

Next, he read the latest Buck Williams report in the cyberzine, *The Truth*. With his contacts around the world, Buck wrote stories that revealed Carpathia's lies without exposing believers who gave Buck information.

Judd was excited when he found a new e-mail from Tsion Ben-Judah. Tsion wrote that he was grateful for the questions he had received at his Web site because it proved many were studying and growing. He spoke of the hope of Christ's return soon and referred to a quote from the apostle Paul who said, "Living is for Christ, and dying is even better."

The next passage disturbed Judd. Tsion wrote that the top priority of believers was not to stop Antichrist from evil.

I want to confound him, revile him, enrage him, frustrate him, and get in the way of his plans every way I know how.

But Tsion said believers should not simply try to fight Carpathia. *Isn't that what we're supposed to do?* Judd thought. The next paragraph answered Judd's question.

So, as worthy and noble a goal as it is to go on the offensive against the evil one, I believe we can do that most effectively by focusing on persuading the undecided to come to faith. Knowing that every day could be our last, that we could be found out and dragged to a mark application center, there to make our decision to die for the sake of Christ, we must be more urgent about our task than ever.

Since many had written about fearing the guillotine, Tsion wrote about his own fears.

In my flesh I am weak. I want to live. I am afraid of death but even more of dying. The very thought of having my head severed from my body repulses me as much as it does anyone. In my worst nightmare I see myself standing before the GC operatives a

*weakling, a quivering mass who can do
nothing but plead for his life. I envision
myself breaking God's heart by denying my
Lord. Oh, what an awful picture!*

*In my most hated imagination I fail at
the hour of testing and accept the mark of
loyalty that we all know is the cursed mark
of the beast, all because I so cherish my
own life.*

Judd closed his eyes and pictured himself
with Global Community Peacekeepers
around him, shoving him toward a guillotine. With the prospect of death, would he
have the courage to say no to Carpathia?
Tsion continued.

*I have good news for you. The Bible tells
us that once one is either sealed by God as a
believer or accepts the mark of loyalty to
Antichrist, this is a once-and-for-all choice.
. . . That tells me that somehow, when we
face the ultimate test, God miraculously
overcomes our evil, selfish flesh and gives us
the grace and courage to make the right
decision in spite of ourselves. My interpreta-
tion of this is that we will be unable to deny
Jesus, unable to even choose the mark that
would temporarily save our lives.*

Judd smiled but was still troubled. If that's true, what happened to Chang?

Judd's computer blipped, and he quickly saved Tsion's message and vowed to read the rest later.

The e-mail was from Chang. *I need to see you. Many questions. Meet me at the gazebo tonight at dusk.*

Judd quickly replied and attached Tsion's latest letter. Though Judd had seen Chang's mark identifying him with Christ, he couldn't help wondering how Chang had Carpathia's mark and what that would do to his soul.

Lionel stood in a corner with Westin and watched the scene unfold. Z-Van and Lars emerged from the isolated room and workers clapped. Z-Van put a hand in the air and waved. "I'm not the hero here. There is one much greater than me coming."

Z-Van rocked back and forth, fidgeting and pulling his head one way and then another until his neck popped. Finally, the elevator opened. Lionel stood on tiptoes, trying to see. There was more clapping and move-ment, and though someone blocked Lionel's view, he sensed evil in the room. Nicolae

Carpathia, the man most of the world worshiped, had arrived.

Lars hurriedly motioned his film crew to begin shooting. Cameras flashed as Carpathia shook hands with Z-Van. "It is my pleasure to welcome you as an honorary Global Community worker, and have you take the mark in the same location as my most loyal followers. Congratulations."

"You don't know what an honor this is, sir," Z-Van said.

"I can only hope the world will want to follow in your footsteps, young man." Carpathia scanned the room, nodding at the workers. "You can see we have a true representation of the world's population in this room. Every ethnic background conceivable is here."

"Very impressive, sir."

Carpathia walked to the mark application area, picked up an injector, and looked into the camera lens. "With this simple device and the application of the mark of loyalty, we will monitor every citizen on earth. Any law-abiding person would be happy to use this technology if it means an outbreak of unparalleled peace, which it does." Carpathia looked at Z-Van. "And I am pleased that a person of your stature and talent wants to show his fans such a moment of leadership."

Z-Van seemed mesmerized by Carpathia. When Nicolae finished, Z-Van nodded and a Peacekeeper took him by the arm and led him to the machine.

Lionel wanted to scream and tell Z-Van not to take the mark, not to sell his soul to the devil, but Lionel knew he was helpless. Z-Van stood spellbound by this enemy of God.

Z-Van sat in a plush chair and scooted against the back. Nicolae smiled and leaned back, allowing the camera to focus on the technician about to apply the mark. The woman looked Filipino and wore gloves. She asked Z-Van a few questions and typed the information into the computer. Since Z-Van was from the United North American States, she set the region code, brushed the hair from Z-Van's forehead, and dabbed at it with a tiny, wet cloth.

With the implanter set, she pressed the device to Z-Van's skin. People around Lionel leaned forward to get a better look. Lionel heard a loud click, then a whoosh.

"Is that it?" Z-Van said.

The woman smiled and nodded. "Now all you need is the identifying mark."

"Give me the number here," Z-Van said, pointing to his forehead.

Carpathia shook the man's hand. "I trust

this will make your music even more enjoyable."

A camera flashed and people around the room clapped. Lionel looked at Westin and shook his head. The procedure had taken only a few seconds and seemed innocent. A person simply received the embedded chip under the skin and a GC number or symbol on the forehead. But those few seconds sealed Z-Van's fate for eternity.

Carpathia held out his hands to the group, looked into the camera, and smiled. "Now, who will be next?"

FIVE

Bi-loyal

JUDD listened to Lionel's story about Z-Van and shuddered. If they had ever hoped he would become a believer, that hope was gone now.

"We got out of there fast," Lionel said. "You think it's safe traveling with a guy who's taken Carpathia's mark?"

"I don't know that the mark means he's under any special mind control. He's just made his final decision."

Westin sighed. "Maybe it's time we all got out. We could get a flight back to the States."

"We still have time," Judd said. "And I really want to be in Israel when Carpathia comes to the Jewish temple."

Near dusk, Judd set out alone for his meeting with Chang. Along the street he saw televisions through shopwindows tuned to the

Global Community Network News. He paused long enough to see footage of Z-Van taking Carpathia's mark. The anchor reported that an anonymous worker inside the Global Community provided the video.

I'll bet Carpathia had someone shoot that himself, Judd thought.

Judd rubbed sweaty palms along his pants as he approached the gazebo. A few uniformed officers strolled the grounds, and several couples talked and laughed on nearby benches. He was in the gazebo only a few minutes when Chang approached, still wearing the red baseball cap.

Chang's face looked tight, and he appeared skittish. Judd reached out to shake his hand, but Chang reached for his cap instead. "You want to see what they did to me?"

Chang whipped off his cap and stared at Judd. The mark of the believer—a cross—was clear. Over it, a small, black tattoo simply read *30.* Beside the number was a half-inch pink scar.

"They say the scar will heal in a few days, but that won't make me look any less like a freak!"

Judd put a hand on Chang's shoulder and led him to a bench. "Don't talk like that."

Chang put a hand to his eyes. "I'm sorry. I

should have listened to you and got out when I could."

"What happened?"

Chang put his hat on and Judd was relieved. He couldn't stop staring at the dual marks.

"My father and one of Carpathia's top men did it. I don't remember much about what happened."

"We saw your father and Moon take you out of the elevator."

"I had another big fight with my father before all this happened. I screamed at him."

"Did you tell him the truth?"

"He and Moon both thought I was upset about getting a shot. They laughed and made fun of me because I was afraid of the needle. I have no idea what I said or did on the way to get the mark. You're looking at the newest hire for the Global Community."

Judd took a breath. "What does the *30* mean?"

"There are ten different regions or sub-potentateships, as Carpathia likes to call them. Dr. Ben-Judah calls them kingdoms like it says in the Bible. There are ten different prefixes, all related to Carpathia, that people will get around the world. I get a *30* because I'm from the United Asian States."

When Chang put his head back, Judd

couldn't help staring at the two marks. He had never seen anything so bizarre.

"I'm so confused," Chang said. "I met with Director Hassid, the believer."

"What did he say?"

"I was still woozy when they took me to him. I tried to act cool, like I was sure of myself, but I really wasn't."

"What aren't you sure about?"

"The Bible says nothing can separate us from the love of Christ. God says we're hidden in the hollow of his hand and that no one can pluck us out. But it also says those who take the mark will be separated from God forever."

"But you didn't choose it—they forced it on you."

"True, but I have doubts. Maybe I'm some kind of freak, like a werewolf. Maybe when the moon's full, I'll follow Carpathia and rat on all my friends."

"You know you won't do that."

Chang leaned forward and put his elbows on his knees. "It's not just my spiritual health. I'm worried about this new position too."

"What do you mean?"

"The believers on the inside of the Global Community have to get out. They want me to come with them—"

"You have to go," Judd interrupted.

"Not if I have this," Chang said, pointing to his forehead. "Carpathia loyalists can't see the mark of the believer. They just see the 30. That means I can live freely among them, buy and sell, and even work here without the slightest suspicion that I'm anything but true-blue GC. Mr. Hassid called it being bi-loyal."

"So you could stay and do what Mr. Hassid has been doing."

"He said I'd never get his job. I'm too young to be a director. But if he teaches me everything he's done inside—listening in on Carpathia, his staff, and warning believers—I could be a big help to the Tribulation Force."

"Sounds like a lot of pressure."

"It won't be very long before Christ comes back. I want to do something worthwhile, even if there's danger."

Judd smiled. He felt the same way, and he was sure others in the Young Tribulation Force did too.

"Mr. Hassid wants me to keep playing things cool until I'm offered the job in his department."

"That way they won't suspect you when he shows up missing, right?"

Chang nodded.

"How are they going to escape?"

"I can't tell you that. It's not that I don't trust you. I just have to keep their secret."

"Understood. It must be exciting thinking about being alone in your own place. I assume your parents are going back to China."

Chang nodded again.

"Have they taken the mark yet?"

"No, and it's curious. I saw Z-Van was allowed to take it. I thought my father would have pulled a few strings to get him and my mother inside to get theirs as well."

"Maybe you can convince them not to do it," Judd said.

"I pray every hour that they will not take the mark."

After much debate about whether the GC would recognize Vicki, she convinced the others to allow her to be the decoy inside the reeducation facility. She changed clothes and rode with Colin and the others in the van. Colin had asked Jim Dekker and Natalie Bishop to send immediate orders to Iowa, and Dekker gave them phone numbers and names for the leaders there. "I'll have everyone pray for you," Jim Dekker had said.

They were a few miles away when Mark and Pete pulled the van and the truck to the roadside. Everyone got out, joined hands, and prayed that God would show them what to do.

When they were finished, Colin looked at Vicki. "I'm not comfortable taking you inside the facility. I'll go in alone as Commander Blakely and take my chances."

Vicki shook her head. "I can get inside, identify all the believers, and get out. Plus I can tell them what's going on. It'll lend credibility to your story."

"If something goes wrong . . ."

"You won't be able to get me out. But it's the same for you. I don't want to have to go back to Wisconsin and tell your wife we let you die here."

Pete held up a hand and put an arm around Colin. "You haven't known these kids as long as I have. They're about as fearless as anybody I've ever known."

Vicki smiled.

"And they're reckless and irresponsible at times," Pete added.

"Why would you say a thing like that?" Shelly said.

"Because it's true." Pete looked at Colin again. "But I know one thing. God's working through them. I've seen it happen before, and I don't doubt that he's going to work through them again."

Colin pursed his lips and nodded. "Okay. Keep your radio on."

Pete drove ahead of them, making sure he had his papers for the injection devices. Mark drove to within a few hundred yards of the entrance to the facility, which was ringed with chain-link fencing and barbed wire around the top.

The kids waited while Pete made his delivery. Colin talked with Jim Dekker and verified that the transfer order for Judah-ite prisoners had been sent from the Des Plaines office.

As Pete's truck pulled away from the facility, he radioed the van. "Package delivered and ready. He is risen."

Colin dialed the number of the Iowa facility and identified himself as Commander Blakely. "You should have received a transfer request for a few of your prisoners. We've captured a suspected Judah-ite, and she's given us information about others in this area. . . . Yes, they're real squealers when you threaten them with the right punishment. . . . No, we'll be taking them with us—"

Colin frowned and closed his eyes. "Let me remind you that you're speaking to a superior officer. I say we're taking them with us. We're pulling up to your facility now, and I expect complete compliance."

Colin hung up the phone. "I hope this works."

Shelly found a pair of handcuffs Jim Dekker had included with their stash of uniforms and equipment. Vicki put her hands behind her, and Shelly quickly locked the cuffs around her wrists. "It's not too uncomfortable, is it?"

Vicki smiled. "You're supposed to be GC. You don't care how it makes me feel."

Mark got past the front gate guard by showing their fake papers. Though the road to the buildings wasn't paved, the main facility looked new. It was two stories and shaped like a U.

Mark parked the van in front and Colin turned to Vicki. "What I say or do to you in there is for your protection. Understand?"

Vicki nodded. "You're the commander, sir. I'm the prisoner."

Colin looked at the others. "The rest of you stay outside the van and wait for me. I'll signal if there's a problem. And if there is, get out of here as fast as you can."

Colin pulled Vicki out roughly, and she nearly fell on the concrete stairs that led to the main building. A man in a deputy commander's uniform walked out quickly and saluted Colin. Vicki kept her head down.

"Like I said on the phone, sir," the deputy

commander said, "we're ready to process the prisoners—"

"Then I'm glad we got here in time. If you'll show me where you're holding the prisoners, we'll let this one identify her friends and be on our way."

"Sir, we've been waiting all day to begin—"

"Have I not made myself clear, Deputy Commander?" Colin said forcefully. "We have reason to believe some of your prisoners will choose the blade instead of the mark of loyalty."

"All the better," the man said. "We'll be done with them."

"Have you ever heard of Tsion Ben-Judah? Have you not been briefed on the Tribulation Force? One of your prisoners may know the location of the Judah-ites' main hideout. If my superiors or anyone in New Babylon finds out that you've hindered the process—"

"I'm sorry, sir. I understand. Right this way."

Colin took Vicki's arm and rushed her up the stairs, following the deputy commander closely. GC guards stood at the doorway with guns. As she entered, she glanced back at her friends. Shelly gave her a nod as Colin pushed Vicki into the enemy's lair.

SIX

Vicki's Meeting

VICKI felt the eyes of the GC guards on her as soon as she walked into the building. There was a sense of evil about the place. These were people who had given their lives to the Global Community, pledged their service to Nicolae Carpathia, and would no doubt kill believers without a second thought.

"It's a shame these prisoners get to take the mark of loyalty first," the deputy commander said. "I've got a whole staff here anxious to go."

Colin bristled and spoke softly to the man. "Those orders are from New Babylon, and I'll caution you not to spread dissention among your workers."

"I only meant that—"

"I know what you meant, and I commend you for wanting to show your devotion. But a subtle complaint like that can infect those around you and cause people to question the ultimate authority of the potentate."

The deputy commander stopped. "I would never want that, sir. Please forgive my lapse in judgment."

Colin nodded and put out a hand. "Proceed."

The deputy commander gleefully reported that they had received information from around the country and the world of many successful mark applications. "We haven't heard one story of applicators failing."

"Any news about those who wouldn't take the mark?"

"There have been a few pockets of resistance. We raided an underground meeting in Arizona and found Judah-ites. Every one of them chose the blade instead of—"

"Please refer to it as a loyalty enforcement facilitator," Colin corrected.

"Of course. Sorry, sir. There have been Judah-ite . . . uh, deaths in the south and northeast as well. North Carolina. Maryland. Pennsylvania. I suppose you saw the communiqué from New Babylon about this."

"I haven't yet. What did it say?"

They walked through a series of doors, and Vicki felt a whoosh of air as she walked inside one of the long buildings attached to the main one. The farther they went, the more scared Vicki became. *What if they find out Colin's not GC?*

"The report listed the number of uses of the loyalty enforcement facilitators. They seemed to be concentrated in the United Asian States and, believe it or not, in the United Carpathian States."

"How could that be?" Colin said. "I had heard the UCS had the lowest concentration of rebels than any other region."

"You would think so," the deputy commander said. "But they rounded up a large contingent in Ptolemaïs, in the country formerly known as Greece."

"And took care of the problem?"

The deputy commander ran a finger across his neck. "With one chop."

The man opened a final door that led into the holding area. "I assumed you wanted to go to the women's facility first."

Colin scratched his chin. "That's fine."

"How did you catch this one?"

"She was helping a group of Judah-ites store food and medical supplies. She has agreed to identify the rebels in this group in exchange for leniency in her sentence."

"Is that right?" the deputy commander sneered.

Colin leaned over to the man and whispered something.

The man laughed. "A Judah-ite rat, eh? If you ask me, they're all like rats, spreading betrayal to the potentate like a disease."

Colin unlocked her handcuffs and leaned toward Vicki. "Find as many of them as you can and do it quickly, Judah-ite."

Vicki glared at Colin as the deputy commander shoved her inside. "Find them or it's the blade for you."

Vicki walked inside the open area of the women's division. A thin carpet, marked in places with colored tape, covered the floor. She guessed this was where prisoners lined up each morning.

The room was lit with natural light from several skylights. Bars covered doors and windows along the walls. Vicki noticed several cameras overhead focusing on different parts of the building.

Vicki guessed there were a few hundred women in the long room. Many were teenagers or in their early twenties who had somehow run afoul of the Global Community. Some had hardened faces, while others seemed lost, frightened, and confused. Though this building was larger, it reminded her of her stay in the Northside Detention Center.

Women milled about the room in clusters, talking and laughing. Some lay on the floor while others exercised, power-walking the length of the room.

A hush fell over the crowd when they saw Vicki. A woman motioned for her to come closer. "You got any smokes?"

Vicki shook her head and walked through the crowd, looking for anyone with the mark of the believer. As she passed, she overheard a few women talking about the mark. "Those kids said if we let the GC put that chip in and give us the tattoo, we can't get into heaven."

"You don't have to worry about getting into heaven," another laughed. "You'd never make it anyway."

Several women laughed.

"Excuse me," Vicki said. "What girls were talking about not taking the mark?"

A tall blonde woman stepped forward. "Did we invite you into this conversation?"

"I'm just looking for—"

"I don't care who you're looking for. Don't interrupt!"

Vicki glanced back and saw Colin and the deputy commander moving into another room. She knew she didn't have much time, but in a group this large, it could take a while to find all of the believers.

As Vicki moved forward, a woman took her arm and whispered, "Don't be afraid of Donna. The girls you're looking for are in the back corner."

Vicki found two groups of believers surrounded by a cluster of inmates. The girls saw the mark on her forehead and rushed to her. Vicki quickly explained she had met them at the college and was here to help. A few women without the mark inched closer.

"I don't have much time. They're going to start processing people for the mark in a little while."

One girl shook her head. "They wheeled the guillotine through this morning. I thought we were goners."

"You kids aren't thinking of refusing the mark, are you?" a woman at the edge said.

A dark-haired girl spoke up. "We've been trying to tell you, if you take Carpathia's mark, you've sealed your fate for eternity."

The woman rolled her eyes and shook her head. "Religious crazies," she muttered.

"I need to identify all the believers for the GC," Vicki said. "How many are there?"

"Three guys and ten girls as far as we know," the dark-haired girl said.

"What about Cheryl?" another girl said.

"Who's Cheryl?" Vicki said.

"In the corner with her back to us," the dark-haired girl said. "We've held meetings to try and tell people the truth. Cheryl seems really interested, but she hasn't made up her mind yet."

"She'd better hurry," Vicki said.

Another believer talked with Cheryl about the Bible but seemed frustrated. Then Vicki approached, sat, and took Cheryl's hand. "My name's Vicki Byrne. Someone said you're pretty interested in what these girls have been saying."

Cheryl nodded. She was small framed, had blonde hair, and wore a sweater. Vicki guessed she was about sixteen. The girl's eyes were puffy and red.

Cheryl wiped away a tear. "I want to believe what they say, but I don't think God could love me."

Vicki stared at the girl, bit her lip, and began. "I never rush people into a decision like this, but we're in a big hurry. The Global Community wants you to take a mark of loyalty to Carpathia, and if you do that, you won't be able to accept God's truth."

"I've been really bad."

"I understand. I was no angel before I

found out about God. But it doesn't matter how bad or good you are, because all it takes is one sin to separate us from God. That's why he sent his Son to die in our place and take the punishment for our sins."

"You mean, Jesus?"

"Right. In the Bible it says that anyone who receives him has eternal life. But the people who reject him, reject God himself."

"But that's not what the Global Community wants us to believe."

Someone blew a whistle at the other end of the room and Vicki stood. She looked through the masses of women and girls and saw Colin with the deputy commander.

Vicki knelt by Cheryl. "I'm going to pray a prayer because I have to go. If you want, you can say it with me or have one of the other girls pray with you. This is how you receive God's gift."

The whistle blew again, and the deputy commander yelled for everyone to sit on the floor.

"God in heaven, I know that I have sinned against you and I deserve to be punished," Vicki whispered. "I want to turn from my sin right now and receive the gift you're offering me. I believe Jesus came to die for my sins so that I could be forgiven, and that he was raised again so that I might spend eternity with you. Right now I want to reach out to you and ask you to be the Lord of my life. Forgive me. Save me. In Jesus' name, amen."

Vicki glanced at Cheryl's forehead, but there was no mark of the believer. "You still have questions?"

"How did you know?"

Vicki smiled. "It's written on your face."

Vicki glanced toward the center of the room and saw Colin and the deputy commander moving through the crowd of women. "I have to go. Please pray that prayer. And no matter what you do, don't take the mark of Carpathia."

Colin grabbed Vicki by the arm and pulled her to a standing position. "Have you found them?" he screamed.

Vicki nodded. "I don't know all their names, but I can show you which ones they are."

"She's a traitor!" the tall blonde woman yelled.

The deputy commander turned and called for silence. "There will be none of that." He looked at Vicki. "Point out the Judah-ites."

Vicki looked at Colin and gave a harried glance toward Cheryl and the dark-haired girl, who were still talking in the corner.

"Let's come back here after she's seen the males," Colin said.

Natalie Bishop was double-checking the progress at the Iowa reeducation facility to make sure the order she had sent had gone through. She had used Deputy Commander Henderson's computer while he was out earlier and had typed in Colin's fake name, Commander Blakely, as the ordering officer.

As the afternoon had worn on and she hadn't heard from Vicki or the others, she had become worried. What if she had led them into a trap? What if the deputy commander in Iowa hadn't gotten the release order for the Judah-ites?

Just settle down and stay calm, Natalie told herself.

When Henderson left and told his secretary he wouldn't be returning for the day, the woman gathered her things and walked out the door. Natalie waited, then returned to the office, got on the computer, and pulled up information about the Iowa facility.

She had just called up the release order when Deputy Commander Henderson walked into the office.

"What are you doing?" Henderson said.

Vicki wasn't allowed into the men's section of the prison. Instead, she stood at a window while men filed past. As Vicki pointed out the three believers, GC guards separated them from the other prisoners and led them to a holding room, where they were handcuffed and their names recorded.

One of the younger boys thought he was being led to the mark application site, and the guards had to restrain him. When a guard said he was being turned over to a commander, the boy stared at Colin.

Colin leaned forward and said, "Tell me the truth. Are you a Judah-ite?"

The boy nodded. "How did you know?"

Colin smiled. "Your friends have given you up. But if you will tell us what we want to know, you will live."

Colin gave the order to lead the three males outside to the van. Vicki was taken back to the women's building, and the females were paraded past her like the men had been. When the girls she had known from the abandoned college walked past, she pointed and they were taken into another holding room.

Vicki couldn't help thinking that she was

somehow controlling the destinies of these women. If she chose them, they would be safe from the Global Community. If she let them pass, they would be forced to take the mark of Carpathia. She only chose the believers, of course, but she still felt bad for the women who had rejected God's love.

As the line dwindled, Vicki scanned the crowd for the dark-haired girl she had seen when she first arrived. Finally, when the last few women passed, Vicki spotted her and pointed.

The last girl in line was Cheryl. She had pulled the hood of her sweater over her head. When she passed Vicki, she threw the hood off and Vicki gasped. On Cheryl's forehead was the mark of the true believer.

SEVEN

Natalie's Choice

NATALIE quickly clicked Deputy Commander Henderson's computer off and moved away from his desk.

"I said, what are you doing in here?"

"I'm sorry, sir . . . your computer is so much faster—"

"You have no right." Henderson clicked the computer back on.

"Sir, I was just composing a message to . . . a friend of mine, and I didn't want anybody to see it."

"A love interest?" Henderson said.

Natalie looked away.

Henderson studied the screen. "Let me ask you again, and this time don't lie—"

"I was helping a friend," Natalie interrupted.

"But why were you using *my* computer?

Unless . . ." Henderson pulled up the last document in the computer, and Natalie closed her eyes. If he found the entry about Commander Blakely, the kids were dead.

She fell to the floor and grabbed at her throat, pretending to choke. She glanced at the wall and found the computer's power cord. Before she could reach it, Henderson's foot came down hard on her arm, grinding it into the floor. Natalie cried out, but Henderson kept his eyes on the computer.

"I've had my suspicions about you." He grabbed her arm and pulled her into a chair. "No one can see your computer from your desk. Why would you use mine?"

Natalie rubbed her arm and stared at the man. Before she could speak, he opened the order sent to the Iowa reeducation facility. The name *Commander Blakely* appeared on the screen.

Henderson turned wildly. "Did you send this order from my computer?"

Natalie put her head down and prayed that God would somehow intervene on her behalf.

Henderson pulled out his service revolver and pointed it at Natalie. With the other hand he picked up the phone and dialed. "Send two guards to my office at once." He stared at his computer, then looked hard at

Natalie. "If you sent this order, then you must have been behind the escape of that teenage boy. . . ."

Natalie sat still, trying to come up with a verse about feeling peaceful in a time of great stress. All she could think of was a passage from Isaiah Jim Dekker had included with his last e-mail: *"But Lord, be merciful to us, for we have waited for you. Be our strength each day and our salvation in times of trouble."*

Natalie had wondered how it would feel to be caught. There was a chance she could still talk her way out of this or come up with some kind of explanation, but the more Henderson questioned her, the more her hopes faded. She had helped the Shairtons, Maggie, and the new believer, Manny, escape from the Global Community's snare. She had also helped Vicki, Darrion, and other Young Tribulation Force members. If the plan in Iowa went through, more lives would be saved. *Not bad for a lowly Morale Monitor,* she thought.

The elevator dinged.

Henderson seemed deep in thought. Then he said, "If you sent this order, then Commander Blakely is phony. And if that's true, those four people he took from here are loose." He slammed his hand on the desk. "How could I have been so stupid!"

"If that's true and you report it, you admit your incompetence," Natalie said. "Those orders were placed from your computer. How will anyone know it wasn't you who made Blakely up?"

Two guards rushed into the room and saluted. Henderson set his jaw firmly. "This Morale Monitor is to be held in a private cell until we can interrogate her further."

"What's the charge, sir?" one guard said as he snapped handcuffs on Natalie.

"Treason," Henderson snapped. "And I suspect her to be a Judah-ite."

As they led Natalie to the elevator, she heard Henderson on the phone with someone at the Iowa facility. She prayed that Vicki and the others were already out.

Vicki and the group of believers were led through a side door into an outside holding area. She looked past several GC guards to the van in front of the building. Mark walked toward her and nodded. His eyes widened as the believers were herded through the door. They both knew the van would only hold fifteen people. Counting Colin and the others, there were nineteen. Mark went back to the van and said something into his radio.

The deputy commander and Colin walked outside to count heads. "I don't think you have enough room in your vehicle for these, Commander."

"I'm not interested in their comfort during the ride," Colin said sharply. "We'll manage. Now, if you'll open the gate, we'll be on our way."

Vicki sidled up to the dark-haired girl. "The Morale Monitors at the van are believers too," she whispered. "Tell the others to act like you're upset that I ratted you out."

The girl whispered the message to the others, and it spread through the group.

The deputy commander nodded toward a guard by the chain-link fence, and the man unlocked the gate and slid it back.

Vicki pushed her way to the front, and one by one the kids walked to the van. "You said you'd take me separately!" Vicki yelled.

Conrad shoved Vicki hard. She lost her balance and went down in the gravel.

"Leave her!" the deputy commander said.

The others piled into the van, some grumbling about Vicki, others complaining about how packed the van was. A few had to sit on the floor to fit inside.

"Why don't you leave her here?" the

deputy commander said to Colin. "We would be glad to take care of her for you."

Colin picked Vicki up by one arm, and she screamed in mock pain. "You're not putting me in there with those people. They'll kill me!"

Colin shoved Vicki toward the van and she climbed inside. "She may be able to tell us more."

A guard yelled that the deputy commander had a phone call. The man shook hands with Colin and went inside the building.

Colin closed the door and turned to Mark. "Get us to the main road as quickly as you can."

Mark pulled out, the tires spinning in the gravel. A boy behind Vicki said, "I want to thank you guys for helping us get out of there, but next time I'd like to order a bus."

A few laughed nervously. Colin said, "Keep it down. We're not out of this yet."

"That guy is running toward us!" someone yelled from the back of the van.

Vicki glanced in a side mirror and saw the deputy commander waving his hands, yelling at the guards, and pointing toward the van.

"What do you want me to do?" Mark said, taking his foot from the gas pedal.

"The guards have their guns out!" a girl yelled.

"Step on it!" Colin yelled. "Everybody get down!"

As the van sped toward the front gate, a shot shattered the back window. Kids screamed and Colin told them to stay calm.

"What if they shoot at the gas tank and make it explode?" Shelly screamed.

"That only happens in the movies," Mark said.

The guards at the front scrambled to action, activating a large gate that slowly blocked the entrance.

"Pete, we need some help!" Mark yelled into the radio.

"I'm on my way."

The guards flew inside the guardhouse as the van careened around the closing gate, sending sparks flying. When Mark turned onto the main road, Vicki felt the van tip slightly, and she thought they were going over. Mark swerved and the van righted itself.

"GC cruisers are following us!" someone shouted.

"Okay, here comes Pete," Mark said, slowing.

"What are you doing?" Colin yelled. "Keep going."

Mark stopped the van as Pete's truck neared the entrance. Vicki craned her neck and saw the two guards in front raise their rifles and fire at the truck, then run away. Pete's trailer slid sideways, crashing into the guardhouse and blocking the entrance. The trailer tipped but didn't turn over. GC cruisers raced after them.

Mark put the van in reverse and zoomed toward Pete. The man had a huge gash over one eye and a bruise was forming on his forehead, but he had managed to limp to the middle of the road. Vicki threw open the van door when Mark slowed enough for Pete to climb inside.

Pop-pop-pop went the rifle fire as Vicki slammed the door. Two of the side windows shattered as Mark floored the accelerator and sped away.

"Stay down!" Colin said.

"I don't know where this road comes out," Mark yelled. "We came in the other way."

"Keep going," Pete gasped. "When you come to the next road, turn right."

"Are you all right?" Vicki said.

Pete was on the floor, wedged between a seat and the door. He was holding his right arm and for a moment let go. A dark, red stain covered his shirtsleeve.

"He's bleeding!" Vicki gasped.

One of the kids ripped a piece of cloth from his shirt and tied it around Pete's arm.

The man looked pale and was having a hard time catching his breath.

"Will they be able to trace your truck?" Colin said.

Pete shook his head. "It's under a different name."

"What happened back there?" Shelly yelled.

"I knew that phone call wasn't a good sign," Colin said. "Somebody finally figured out we're not who we said we are."

"You could have fooled us, sir," a boy in the back of the van said.

Colin smiled. He dialed Jim Dekker in Illinois to update him and see if he knew how the GC had discovered them.

Vicki leaned over and put a hand on Pete's forehead. He was breathing easier now, and some of the color had come back to his face. "You hang on until we can get you some help."

Pete smiled. Someone in the back folded a uniform and passed it forward. Vicki placed it under Pete's head, and the big man closed his eyes.

Colin hung up and shook his head. "Jim has no idea how the GC found out about us. He's been trying to get in touch with Natalie, but he can't reach her at her apartment, the jail, or by e-mail."

"You don't think . . . ," Vicki said.

Colin kicked the dashboard with a foot. "I knew she should have gotten out of there."

"We have to go back for her," Vicki said.

"We have to get out of here first," Mark said.

Colin remained silent. "We'll go back and help her, right?"

When no one responded, Vicki slumped onto the floor. She felt helpless, useless.

"Maybe Natalie ran," Shelly said. "She's smart. Maybe she's on her way to Wisconsin right now."

Vicki closed her eyes and prayed that Shelly was right. But something inside her said she wasn't.

Natalie sat on the bunk in her cell, her head in her hands. By now she was sure they had found the e-mails she had sent from Deputy Commander Henderson's computer as well as from Peacekeeper Vesario's machine. Her prayer was that Vicki and the others had gotten away safely.

Natalie leaned against the concrete wall. She had longed to be away from the Global Community, on the outside with Vicki and the others, but she believed God could use her best inside. She had felt a sense of mission, working against the GC, and now her mission was complete.

Natalie regretted not being able to talk to Vicki about her story. She had imagined them sitting on a couch in front of a fire with mugs of hot chocolate steaming in their hands. Vicki would first fill in all the missing places of her story, and then she would listen to Natalie's.

But that wouldn't happen now. Natalie would never have the chance to tell Vicki about the woman who had taught her Sunday school class, who had prayed for Natalie and her family. After the disappearances, Natalie had rushed to the woman's house. When there was no answer at the door, she went inside. The woman's prayer journal was open on the kitchen table, and Natalie found her name. She also found Christian books and literature that she shoved into a garbage bag and dragged home.

Natalie smiled as she thought about how hungry she was for information in those days. She nearly inhaled the books and stayed up all hours of the night reading her Bible and asking God to show her his plan.

"Thank you, God, for using me to help others," she prayed softly.

Natalie suddenly sat up straight, realizing that someone else needed to hear the message. She banged on her cell and yelled for the guard.

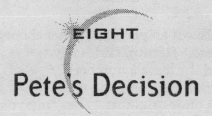

EIGHT

Pete's Decision

VICKI and the others in the van raced through back roads of Iowa, knowing their chances of escaping the GC dragnet were slim if they didn't get help.

Colin dialed Jim Dekker's phone and reached him at the satellite operations center. "They've gotten a request to track us," Colin told the kids a few minutes later.

"Then Jim can help us," Vicki said.

Colin shook his head. "An operator is trying to track us now. Jim doesn't think he can help without revealing himself."

"What about the girl who wrote us, Kelly Bradshaw?" Vicki said. "Maybe she has a place we can hide."

Vicki dialed the Wisconsin safe house and Darrion answered. "No time to talk. We need to get in touch with Kelly Bradshaw."

"I just got an e-mail from her about an hour ago," Darrion said.

"Did she leave a number?"

Darrion pulled up the message and gave Vicki a phone number. "She wants you guys to call her no matter what happens."

Vicki immediately dialed Kelly. The girl was overjoyed to hear they had gotten their friends out safely. Vicki explained the situation and told her they were coming near a more populated area.

Kelly covered the phone and spoke with someone else in the room.

"Tell her we don't have much time," Mark said. "They'll probably have helicopters out soon."

"Hide the van and we'll come get you," Kelly said.

"Where could we hide a big van like this?"

"There!" Colin yelled.

Vicki saw a long, white building with what looked like several hundred garages. On top was a sign that said "U-Store It."

Mark pulled into the parking lot, and Colin told everyone to stay down while he went inside. Vicki gave Kelly the address of the building, and Kelly said they would be there as soon as possible.

"What about Pete?" Shelly said. "We need to get him to a doctor."

"I just need to rest," Pete said. "I think the bleeding's stopped."

Colin motioned for Mark to drive the van around back. He opened one of the large bay doors, and the van barely fit inside. As the others got out and stretched, Vicki covered Pete with some spare uniforms.

Several kids knelt in prayer in the darkened storage room, thanking God for delivering them from sure death at the hands of the GC. They all prayed for Pete and that they would be able to escape the oncoming GC manhunt.

"What did you tell the guy at the front desk?" Vicki asked Colin.

"I told him the truth. The GC is looking for some escapees from a reeducation facility not far from here and to keep his eyes open. I deputized him and told him to—"

Colin stopped as noise filled the storage facility. It grew so loud that the door shook.

"Helicopter," Mark said.

Natalie waited in her cell, praying that her request would be granted. She had promised to tell the GC everything about herself if she could meet with her roommate. She imagined Deputy Commander Henderson mulling over the request, thinking of some way to salvage his career.

An hour passed before a guard handcuffed her and led her to an upstairs interrogation room. "Please, God," she prayed, "I just want to tell Claudia the truth. I know she's been pro-Carpathia ever since we've been roommates, but I've never told her what I really believe. Give me the chance today."

Claudia Zander was tall, blonde, and caught the eye of every male Morale Monitor in the building. Natalie had noticed a slight change in the girl's behavior in the past week. She seemed moody, and the two had talked late one night. Natalie had asked questions but didn't offer any information about her own beliefs.

Natalie heard a door close in the observation room behind her as Claudia walked in. No doubt Henderson and his crew were back there listening. She would give them an earful.

"Thanks for coming," Natalie said.

"I couldn't believe it when I heard. They say you're a Judah-ite and you helped people escape."

"I knew they'd ask you about me, and I wanted to make sure they don't suspect you."

Claudia scooted back from the table. "You can't be serious. You're really working with the enemy?"

"Let me explain." Natalie began at the disappearances and told Claudia how she had come to know the truth about God. When the kids in the Young Tribulation Force had gotten into trouble, she helped.

Natalie leaned forward and whispered, "I want you to know how to begin a relationship with God. All you have to do is pray and ask him to forgive—"

"Shut up!" Claudia looked at the mirror behind Natalie. "I want out of here. She's not telling me anything about the ones who escaped."

Natalie wished she could touch the girl or give some gesture of kindness, but her hands were cuffed behind her. "At least look up the Young Trib Force Web site."

Claudia shook her head and scowled. "You're crazy. I don't know how you could betray all of us like this, but you'll pay."

A guard opened the door and Claudia ran out. Deputy Commander Henderson walked in, smiling. "We have your little group cornered in Iowa. It won't be long now. And since you're being charged with a crime against the Global Community, you're now a prisoner. You know what that means."

Natalie stared at the man. "Sir, I want you to know I'm sorry I misled you. I've lied to you in order to make sure my friends stayed free. But I'm finally ready to tell the truth."

Henderson pulled the chair around and straddled it. "I'm listening."

"God loves you so much, he was willing to die for you. . . ."

When the helicopter passed overhead, Vicki and the others gathered around Colin. "Jim was able to shut the power down at the satellite building briefly so we were able to hide before they located the van. That's the good news. Of course, they're still looking."

"If we don't show up on the satellite, they'll figure we're hiding," a girl said. "Won't they check here at some point?"

Colin nodded. "That's why we need to get this van back on the road. I'll take it and leave you—"

"No way," Vicki interrupted. "You have a wife back in Wisconsin."

"I'm also the senior member of this group."

"Which is another reason you shouldn't go," Mark said.

"They're right," Conrad said. "One of us should do it."

Colin shook his head. "What if we

convince the guy at the front desk to drive it somewhere?"

"The GC will be all over him," Vicki said.

"But he's a Carpathia lover. You should have seen his face light up when he saw my uniform."

Vicki bit her lip. She and Darrion had tricked a man in Des Plaines and it still haunted her. "I don't like getting others mixed up in our problems. What if he has a change of heart and wants to trust God? He'll remember how we treated him."

Mark took off his watch. "What if we give him The Cube and tell him not to look at it until he gets to his destination?"

Vicki scowled. "Sounds like a cop-out."

"All right, you have a better idea?" Mark said.

Vicki shook her head.

"Then it's settled," Colin said. "Write the note."

Vicki mingled with the new kids, asking their names and where they were from. The newest believer, Cheryl Tifanne, was from Des Moines. Global Community Peacekeepers had arrested her for stealing food from a grocery store. "I've been so hungry lately. Sometimes I can find a place in line at one of the shelters, but recently I haven't had much luck."

"We'll make sure you get enough to eat," Vicki said.

Vicki phoned Darrion in Wisconsin and asked if she had heard anything from Natalie. Darrion said she hadn't but that she'd watch the Web.

The phone rang a few moments later, and Kelly said they were an hour away. "We just heard about you guys on the radio. Better make sure the people at that storage place aren't listening."

Vicki volunteered to talk with the man at the front. She walked around the building and approached from the other side.

The lobby had two plastic chairs and an old candy dispenser. The carpet looked like it had been through a couple of floods. Paneling covered the walls and every few feet Vicki noticed cobwebs. There was no TV in the office, but the man behind the counter was listening to the radio.

"How's it going?" Vicki said.

The man took his feet off the desk and nearly fell backward. "You scared me. What can I do for you?"

"What's going on with the helicopter and everything?"

"It's a Global Community thing. I can't really say."

"You heard it on the radio?"

"No. I just know, that's all."

Vicki saw a few tapes scattered across the desk. "Do you like country? I sure do."

"Yeah, I got quite a collection here."

"Mind if I listen to one? I'm waiting for some friends to pick me up."

"Sure," the man said. "Take your pick."

Vicki picked up a cassette and popped it in the player. The man said it was one of his favorites. As the music played, Vicki asked more questions and found out the man lived with his wife and small baby a few miles away. The more she learned, the worse she felt about the plan to let him drive the van.

She excused herself, saying she wanted to check on her ride, and walked back to the storage room. "I've got a bad feeling about this. He's really sweet, and he has a wife and baby. What if the GC hurt him?"

Colin sighed. "I don't want anything to happen to him, but if we're caught, we're dead."

Colin's cell phone rang. It was Kelly calling to say they were only a few minutes away.

Natalie sat stone-faced, looking at Deputy Commander Henderson. She had answered all of his questions except ones about other members of the Young Tribulation Force and

where the four escaped prisoners were hiding. The truth was, she didn't know for sure.
She had purposefully not asked anyone for
the information so she wouldn't have to
lie.

Henderson berated her, accused her of
treason and blasphemy against Potentate
Carpathia.

"I don't argue with any charge except the
last one. You can't blaspheme someone
who's not God."

Henderson seethed, pointing a finger and
asking about the location of the Tribulation
Force's safe house. "You know where this
Ben-Judah is hiding, don't you?"

"I don't, sir, and even if I did, I wouldn't
tell you."

Someone knocked on the door and Henderson slipped outside. Natalie wondered if
these were her last moments. Perhaps they
would question her more or try to torture
information out of her.

She closed her eyes and thought of Zeke
Sr. He had faced Henderson and the others
with such courage. She wondered how he
could possibly do it, but now, instead of feeling anxious and nervous about what was
going to happen, she felt calm. She knew
there was a Bible verse for this, but she
couldn't remember the exact wording. It was

something about Jesus giving peace to everyone who trusts in him.

Natalie sat back, relaxed her arms, and let her head rest on the back of the chair. She had never felt so focused and alive. Though others had the power to take her life, she knew God truly held her destiny in his hands.

"If you rescue me from this, I'll praise you," Natalie whispered. "And if you don't, I'll praise you in heaven. I'm yours, God."

Vicki heard a loud click from the van as Colin raised the door to the storage room. Conrad tried to get in one of the side doors but couldn't. "It's locked!"

The van started and Vicki ran to the front. Pete sat in the driver's seat, his window rolled down a couple of inches.

"Pete, get out of there!" Vicki screamed.

"I agree with what you said about that guy in the front," Pete said, carefully backing out through the open door.

Vicki ran after him but Colin grabbed her. "It's okay. He knows what he's doing."

"You can't let him go! The GC will catch him."

Pete tossed a piece of paper out the

window and waved at the group. Out of the parking lot, he turned left and headed back the way they had come.

Vicki sobbed, tears streaming down her cheeks. "Why did he do that?"

"Because he cares more about us than he does about himself," Mark said. "And he cares about the guy in the office."

Vicki shook her head and prayed that somehow she would be able to see Pete again.

One of the kids handed her the piece of paper from the ground. Her name was scrawled on the front. Vicki stashed the note in her pocket.

NINE

Eyewitness to Bravery

VICKI watched Pete drive out of sight. More vehicles approached from the other direction.

Mark ran toward the office with the note the kids had written. "I'm going to give this to the guy up front!"

A green minivan and two other cars pulled to the back of the storage facility. Vicki recognized Kelly when she got out of the van and hugged her.

"No time for reunions," Colin said. "Everybody get in. Keep some distance between cars and keep in touch with the radios."

Mark hurried out and jumped in the minivan with Vicki, Shelly, Conrad, and several others. The rest filled the cars.

"Did you give the note to him?" Vicki said.

Mark nodded. "I didn't have time to talk. I just told him that there was information he

needed to read and share with his family.
I gave him my watch so he could see The
Cube."

"But he doesn't know how to pray," Vicki
said.

"I put the Web site address on the note. He
has enough information now."

As Kelly drove along the road, Vicki kept
looking behind them and checking overhead.
Several times she thought she heard helicopters, but none appeared.

"Who are the other drivers?" Vicki asked.

"We've known about some older believers
who live a few miles from the school. I ran
there this morning. Two volunteered to
drive, and the rest are praying for us now."

"Where are we going?" Mark said.

"It's better if we split up to different
houses," Kelly said. "Neighbors won't be
suspicious."

"We'll have to go into hiding anyway,"
another girl said. "They'll be giving the mark
to the rest of the population soon."

Vicki knew they were right, but she had
hoped to get back to Wisconsin soon. Natalie
needed to get away from the GC, plus it was
possible Judd and Lionel were coming back.
She didn't want to miss that.

Vicki pulled the bloody paper from her
pocket and held it a moment. She prayed the

GC wouldn't spot Pete and asked God to keep him alive. "We've lost so many already. Don't let us lose Pete."

Vicki took a breath. The bloodstains were mostly on the outside of the paper where Pete had folded it. He had scrawled the note on the back of Colin's fake GC orders for the Iowa prisoners.

> *Dear Vicki,*
>
> *Forgive my shaky handwriting. I agree with what you said about that guy in the office. We shouldn't use others who aren't believers just to keep ourselves safe. We're here to reach out to people who don't know God.*
>
> *That's why I'm leaving with the van. I don't know if I'll escape, but know this. No matter what happens, I'll be waiting for you kids on the other side.*
>
> *Vicki, I want you to know, if I ever had a daughter, I'd want her to be just like you. If your parents can see you from heaven, I know they're looking on with pride. God has planned something special for you. I know that.*
>
> *I'd better stop writing because the people are almost here to pick you up.*
>
> *I love you, Vicki. Tell Judd, Mark, Lionel, and all the others that I feel the same about them. Stay steady. Trust God.*

Celebrate him with abandon every day and never stop telling the truth. Remember, God wins in the end, so we're fighting a defeated enemy.
   Pete

Vicki closed her eyes and let the tears fall. Pete had been like a big brother to her. Having friends like him who cared helped her go on each day.

She shook her head. She wasn't giving up on him. Though he was hurt and vulnerable to the Global Community, she decided not to entertain the idea that she had seen him for the last time. Pete would be back. He had to come back. She folded the paper, shoved it in her pocket, and wiped away the tears.

Mark put a hand on her shoulder and asked if she was okay.

"I'll be all right."

Judd waited for word from Chang as he sat in front of the computer. Lionel and Westin had gone to bed, but Judd couldn't sleep. Z-Van was entertaining guests, so Judd sat at the small desk in the bedroom and put on headphones as he surfed the Internet.

Judd logged on to the official GC Web site

and discovered the numbers of prisoners who had been executed in different areas around the world. He checked the States first and recognized Zeke's father's name from the Des Plaines facility. He felt bad for Zeke and wondered where he was.

There were also several prisoners in Arizona, California, and Texas who had decided against taking Carpathia's mark. Judd scrolled through the different regions and, to his surprise, found that many had chosen the guillotine in the former country of Greece, now part of the United Carpathian States.

Judd was stunned when he found Anton Rudja's name on the list of prisoners who had been executed. Anton Rudja's son was Pavel, Judd's friend who had first invited him to New Babylon.

When he recovered, Judd checked back to the kids' Web site and found an e-mail from Buck Williams.

> *Friends,*
>
> *I'm sending this quick note so you can be the first to know that there are now many martyrs for the faith in Greece. I will write further about the specifics in The Truth when I can complete the story, but know that the believers there were brave.*

The underground church in Ptolemaïs, Greece, was probably the largest in the United Carpathian States. The Greek believers were careful, even though local GC Peacekeepers seemed to look the other way for a while. Sources tell me the reason for the crackdown was that Carpathia wanted the region that bore his name to have the lowest reports of Christ-followers of the ten global supercommunities. Rather than pretend the rebels didn't exist, many were rounded up from local meetings and forced to make a decision for or against Carpathia.

I cannot begin to tell you the amount of courage those believers exhibited. GC authorities tried to scare people by carting guillotines through the streets in open trucks. They're ugly contraptions, and there isn't much to them. Just wood, screws, blade, spring, and rope. They will put these at the mark application sites to make people comply, but if others act the way our brothers and sisters in Greece did, they won't back down.

When prisoners were told they would be taking the mark, people cheered and many young people started chanting and singing about Carpathia. The GC handled the mark application and the biochip injection with great efficiency. It won't surprise me if they

take what they learned here and create a
fast-moving system that will get people in
and out of the process in a few minutes.

I witnessed the most inhuman treatment
of the believers. One woman who knelt to
pray was treated savagely by her captors.
Though she was beaten and bloody, she did
not obey. And as the man who led the
group asked for those who would not take
the mark, more stepped forward, some of
their marks appearing as they raised their
hands to change lines.

When the first woman knelt in front of
that ugly machine, the room fell silent. This
woman began to sing "My Jesus, I Love
Thee" but had only finished a few words
when the blade came down to end her life.

I have never seen such courage, such
resolve, and such bravery. I know we will
see those women again in heaven, but their
deaths, so jarring, have caused me to write
you.

Pray for other believers who may even
now be going through the same fate.

Judd shuddered as he read the rest of
Buck's eyewitness account. He wondered
how Buck had managed to be inside a
prison, but he knew the Tribulation Force
had many contacts in many lands.

He also wondered how many in the next few weeks would unknowingly seal their eternal fate by taking Carpathia's mark. The process would be simple. Get in line, take the biochip and tattoo, and go on with your life. Little did they know that taking the mark meant eternal death, and kneeling before the bloody guillotine was the only other option.

Judd returned to a passage in Tsion Ben-Judah's latest e-mail. Tsion had suggested everyone memorize Revelation chapter 20 and verse 4:

> *"I saw the souls of those who had been beheaded for their testimony about Jesus, for proclaiming the word of God. And I saw the souls of those who had not worshiped the beast or his statue, nor accepted his mark on their forehead or their hands. They came to life again, and they reigned with Christ for a thousand years."*

> *Your loved ones who have been called to what the world would call a gory end shall return with Christ at his Glorious Appearing! Tsion wrote. They shall live and reign with him for a thousand years! Glory be to God the Father and his Son, Jesus the Christ!*

Judd closed his eyes and wondered if he would have to experience the guillotine. The phone rang and he quickly picked it up.

It was Chang. "I need to talk. I'm downstairs in the lobby."

Judd sneaked past the guests in the suite and hurried downstairs. He found Chang sitting on a plush chair, his back to the elevators. Judd sat across from him and stared at the mark on the boy's forehead.

"Can't help yourself, can you?" Chang said.

"I'm sorry. It's just so weird to see both of those together."

Chang shook his head. "It's haunting me. I've been trying to remember what happened—if I resisted or if I just sat down and let them give me the mark. I vaguely remember arguing with my father and a camera flashing in my face, but that's about it."

"Are your parents still here?" Judd said.

Chang nodded. "They leave tomorrow morning. I've convinced them I'm okay and that working for the GC won't be as bad as I thought."

Judd inched closer. "Have they taken the mark?"

"Thankfully, no. I think my father was upset by the whole Z-Van spectacle. He wanted to take the mark while he was here, but now he says they will simply do it when they get back home."

"Are you meeting with Mr. Hassid?"

"We try to talk after hours. We'll be going over the different things he's set up via the computer system here. It looks like I'll be their only contact inside."

Someone walked past and Chang paused. He put a hand to his forehead and sighed. "I don't know if I can do it."

"Of course you can. You're as capable as anybody—"

"It's not that. I know I can do the job. What I don't know is if I can keep it all together."

"I don't understand."

Chang leaned forward and whispered, "These two marks are driving me crazy. When I look in the mirror, all I see is Carpathia's number. I'd like to burn it off or cut it out. I haven't been able to talk with anyone. If I tell Mr. Hassid, he'll think I can't handle the job. If I tell my father, he'll know I'm not loyal to Carpathia and he'll report me."

"What about your mother?"

Chang lowered his head. "I don't know if I should trust her. There are things I can't remember. I think we talked about Ming and me being followers of Ben-Judah, but I'm not sure."

"Your sister is still working inside too?"

Chang shook his head. "She has escaped to the Tribulation Force. How I wish I could be there. I would sit down and talk with Dr. Ben-Judah."

"You'll get your chance," Judd said.

Chang told Judd the inside information he had learned about Carpathia and how angry the potentate was about the Judah-ites. "What about you?" Chang said. "Do you have a safe place to hide?"

"We're not sure it's so safe, but we're going back to Israel with Z-Van's crew."

Chang frowned when Judd told him Lionel's story of Z-Van taking the mark. He looked at his watch and rose to leave.

Judd wanted to say something that would comfort and encourage the boy, but nothing came to mind. He put a hand on Chang's arm. "The only thing I know to tell you is that we'll be praying for you. God keeps his promises, and if you have his mark, he's not going to reject you."

"Are you sure about that?"

Judd watched Chang walk out of the lobby and into the darkened streets. If

Chang stayed in New Babylon, he would likely be the only believer there. It would be one of the loneliest assignments of any in the Tribulation Force.

TEN

The Loss

Vicki awoke the next morning in the basement of a strange house. She felt something crackle as she rolled to a sitting position and found Pete's letter still folded in her front pocket.

Seven kids were staying at this house. Conrad, Mark, and Shelly had joined Vicki in the green minivan after Pete had driven away. Vicki knew the name of only one of the three girls there—Cheryl, the new believer.

Someone coughed in the bathroom nearby. Whoever it was sounded ill. A few minutes later, Cheryl came out of the bathroom holding her stomach. "Must have been something I ate."

Vicki crept upstairs to find medicine for Cheryl and found a group of adults sitting around the kitchen table, all with the mark of the believer. They stopped talking when Vicki walked in. She explained what she was looking for, and a woman hurried to a nearby pantry.

The others stared at Vicki until a younger man standing against the kitchen counter broke the silence. He looked about twenty, was tall and thin, with dark hair. He sipped from a coffee mug and studied Vicki. "I heard we had a celebrity in the house. Aren't you the one from the satellite broadcast?"

Vicki extended a hand. "I'm Vicki Byrne."

The man smiled and shook Vicki's hand warmly. "Chad Harris. Nice to meet you."

"You saw the satellite broadcast?"

"In Des Moines. We drove some believers there to hand out copies of *The Truth.* I assume you know about Buck Williams's reporting?"

Vicki nodded.

"It was impressive what you were able to do. We saw a lot of kids actually get the mark of the believer after your presentation."

Vicki told them about the satellite truck and how Carl Meninger had risked his life in Florida to help them beam the signal to Israel and around the world.

The woman came back with some medicine and said she would go downstairs to help Cheryl.

"Is the Global Community looking for us?" Vicki said nervously.

Chad laughed. "I'd say that's a pretty good guess."

Vicki gritted her teeth. "What I mean is, are there reports about us in the media?"

Chad sobered. "It's been pretty silent about you kids. I don't think the GC wants anybody to know they let you get away."

"What about the others?"

"We have you split up in different houses. You're all safe."

"And Pete? He's the guy who drove the van—"

An older man at the table sat forward. "Haven't heard anything about him yet. We'll let you know if we do. Right now, you need to get back downstairs and relax. We'll take care of you."

Vicki thanked them, and Chad lifted his coffee mug toward her. "If you need anything, just let us know."

Vicki went downstairs to find Mark on the phone with Jim Dekker in Illinois. Mark's face showed the strain of the past two days when he hung up. "Jim was able to keep the power off in the building until the van was hidden. A couple hours later the GC spotted the van heading west and caught up to it before nightfall."

"They have Pete?" Vicki gasped.

"Jim doesn't know. He needs to talk with Natalie to get the information."

"Let's e-mail her."

"He's done that. No answer."

"If they have the van, they'll trace it to Wisconsin, right?"

"Colin took care of that a long time ago. But there's another problem." Mark sat on a couch.

The television was on in the background, and two of the girls from the reeducation facility were watching the latest news. Thousands had gathered near a statue of Nicolae Carpathia in Spain and knelt before it. The report switched to Australia, then to a city in South Africa, where more people worshiped Carpathia.

Mark turned back to Vicki and pursed his lips. "Dekker was supposed to have returned the commander's uniform that Colin's been wearing. Because of this trip, he couldn't."

"So Jim's in trouble," Vicki said, sitting next to Mark.

"They haven't accused him yet, but the operator of the cleaners in Jim's building was taken in for questioning. They must have found out Colin's Commander Blakely was fake and traced the missing uniform."

"Is the guy a believer?"

Mark shook his head. "No, but Jim says he won't let the guy hang for something that's Jim's fault. If he's not released soon, Jim may turn himself in."

Vicki put her head back on the couch and sighed. "That means they'll search Jim's house. Are the Shairtons and the others still there?"

"They were supposed to be on their way to Wisconsin overnight. I checked with Darrion and she said they hadn't made it yet."

Vicki put a hand to her forehead. "Everything's falling apart."

Cheryl came out of the bathroom with Shelly. Shelly gave Vicki a strange look.

"Feel any better?" Vicki said.

"A little. I'm going to rest some more."

When Shelly joined them, Vicki asked her what the look was for. "I'll tell you later," Shelly said.

Conrad called them over to a computer stacked on top of a pool table.

Mark told Vicki that he'd learned something about this house where they were staying. Before the Rapture the people who owned it had several children, one of whom was left behind during the global disappearances. "He opened the house to some of his uncles and cousins. They've been reading Tsion's Web site every day."

"Is Chad the son who was left behind?" Vicki said.

Mark nodded.

"He's pretty cute," Shelly said playfully.

"Watch it," Conrad said. He turned the computer screen where everyone could see it. "I was doing some research too. Look at this information I found buried on the official GC Web site."

A picture showed several people standing in front of a fire, with what looked like a huge church in the background. Vicki inched closer and saw it was the Vatican.

"These are photos of Global Community officers destroying paintings, sculptures, icons, and even old Bibles," Conrad said. "The directive came from Leon Fortunato himself."

Mark shook his head. "That stuff is priceless."

"A spokesman said they destroyed everything that paid tribute to the impotent God of the Bible," Conrad said.

"Pretty soon they're going to see he's not so impotent," Vicki said.

Judd talked with Chang on the phone the next day and discovered that Chang's parents were gone. The GC had offered to let them both take the mark in New Babylon, but Mr. Wong had refused. There had been a tearful good-bye at the airport, and Chang returned to the apartment and was assigned permanent quarters. "I'm all by myself now with my own room and my own computer. I don't have to worry about my parents listening in on my conversations."

"Have you talked with Mr. Hassid about his escape?"

"Sorry, Judd, I can't tell you about that. I can tell you this though. Director Hassid and I are designing a new computer system. I should be able to do everything he did up until now from my office or from here in my new apartment."

"What will you do?"

"I'll give the Tribulation Force access to anything they want to hear or see in the palace. But first, I have to monitor the escape and keep things going in the safe house in Chicago. It's going to be a pretty complex mission."

"Who will be your new boss after Hassid leaves?"

"A guy named Aurelio Figueroa. David says he treats the people above him like kings and queens and the people below him like servants. I should be able to handle him okay."

Judd asked how Chang was doing with his feelings about the dual marks, but the boy quickly changed the subject. "Director Hassid showed me how to tap into both live and recorded conversations in the palace, and I came across something you'll be interested in. Are you ready?"

Judd heard several keyboard clicks, then the unmistakable voice of Nicolae Carpathia. "Now when I spoke the other day of a host of enforcers, I wanted you to gather that I meant the very core of my most loyal troops, the GCMM. They are already armed. I want them supported! I want them fully equipped! I want you to marry them with our munitions so their monitoring will have teeth. They should be respected and revered to the point of fear."

"You want the citizenry afraid, sir?" another man said.

"Walter! No man need fear me who loves and worships me. You know that."

"I do, sir."

"If any man, woman, young person, or child has reason to feel guilty when encountering a member of the Global Community Morale Monitoring Force, then yes, I want them shaking in their boots!"

Chang stopped the recording. "Carpathia's talking with Walter Moon, the new supreme commander. They go on about their budget, and then Carpathia says he's going to have at least one hundred thousand armed troops in Israel when he returns there."

"A hundred thousand?"

"You may want to reconsider going."

"Maybe it's time we head back to the States. It's probably a lot safer."

Vicki and the others were careful to stay inside the rest of the day. All the kids were glad when they received the news that Bo and Ginny Shairton, Maggie Carlson, and Manny Aguilara had made it safely to the hideout in Wisconsin. They had also taken an ample supply of Jim Dekker's uniforms and Global Community gear.

But their joy quickly turned to concern when Jim Dekker phoned. Vicki answered and asked for an update.

"No change with me," Jim said, "but you need to sit down."

"What's wrong?"

"It's about Natalie."

"Is she still in Des Plaines? She should have gotten out of there a long time ago."

"I'm afraid she won't be getting out, Vicki."

"No, even if I have to go down there and—"

"She's gone, Vicki. I just received a communiqué from Des Plaines. That deputy commander over her is being—"

"What do you mean, she's gone?" Vicki interrupted.

"Let me read this release to you. It's to all United North American GC."

Vicki's heart raced as Jim Dekker slowly read the words she dreaded to hear.

> "*Deputy Commander Darryl Henderson was relieved of duty after a Judah-ite plot was discovered under his command. At least four prisoners were released in Des Plaines, and more than a dozen more in Iowa when a man posing as Commander Regis Blakely presented false papers and escorted prisoners out of custody.*
>
> "*It is believed that a female Morale Monitor, Natalie Bishop, 17, aided the impostor by sending information of the transfer via Deputy Commander Henderson's computer.*
>
> "*The Global Community joint chiefs of the United North American States have appointed Commander Kruno Fulcire as head of the Rebel Apprehension Program (RAP). Commander Fulcire will visit the suburban Chicago facility, as well as the Iowa reeducation facility where the escapes took place.*"

"But it doesn't say anything about Natalie's death," Vicki said. "They could still want to interrogate her!"

"Let me finish," Jim said. He took a breath and continued.

> "Commander Fulcire reported that the Morale Monitor Bishop was given the opportunity to swear allegiance to Potentate Carpathia by taking his mark of loyalty. Upon refusal, Peacekeepers used the loyalty enforcement facilitator."

"No," Vicki whispered. She felt like she had been kicked in the stomach. Shelly, Mark, and Conrad kept asking questions, but she waved them off.

"They go on to say they think this is the first Global Community employee to die for not taking Carpathia's mark. Commander Fulcire says this shows the importance of administering the mark to everyone on the planet. He has commanded complete compliance from every Global Community employee."

"Jim, you have to get out of there right now. If you turn yourself in for stealing the uniforms—"

"I'm not letting somebody take the fall for

my actions! Even if he is an unbeliever." Jim clicked at his computer, then gasped.

"What's wrong?"

"They've taken the guy from the cleaners to Des Plaines to give him Carpathia's mark."

"Then you have to get out."

"This is my fault," Jim said. "I have to go. I'll let you know what happens."

"Jim, listen—"

Click.

Mark, Conrad, and Shelly gathered around Vicki, and two others from the reeducation center joined them. Vicki was too overcome to speak, but the others could tell what had happened from the conversation.

"Father, we've lost another member of our team today," Mark said, his voice breaking. "We can only imagine what those last moments were like for Natalie. But you gave her the courage to be faithful to you, even until death."

"We know that one day we'll see her again," Conrad continued, "but right now we're hurting. Show us every step we need to take, and make us brave like Natalie. Amen."

ELEVEN

Chad Harris

VICKI spent a few hours alone, thinking about Natalie, how they had met, and what the girl had done for the Young Trib Force. They wouldn't have escaped the schoolhouse or gotten Charlie and the others away from the Global Community without her. Vicki cried herself to sleep and had nightmares about the guillotine.

When Vicki woke up the next morning, she didn't want to talk with anyone. Turning over in bed, she grabbed a Bible, leafed through the pages, and closed it.

"God, I don't know why you let this happen. You saved people before, you helped us get out safely, but you let Natalie die. Why? I don't understand."

Vicki buried her face in her pillow and wept. She wanted to blame someone for

Natalie's death, but she couldn't shake the feeling that the girl had died because of Vicki's choices.

While Z-Van and his group went into a studio to record, Judd and Lionel went with Westin Jakes to Z-Van's plane at the New Babylon airport. Though they were able to talk at the hotel, they all felt freer on the airplane.

The three prayed about their next move, feeling strongly that they should get out of New Babylon. But they didn't know whether they would travel to Israel or the States.

"The truth is," Judd said, "you may have to get out before we do."

"Why?" Westin said.

"Z-Van has already taken the mark. His fate is sealed. But you know he's going to want everyone around him to take the mark. Working for him might be worse than being inside the GC."

Westin frowned. "Ever since I prayed to God, I've known that my days with Z-Van were short. I guess I didn't want to think about it."

"If all three of us leave together, we could

fly commercial back to the States," Lionel suggested.

Westin frowned again. "Is it wrong to take an airplane like this?"

"You mean steal it?" Judd said.

Westin nodded. "We could really use this thing for the Young Trib Force."

Lionel sighed. "Maybe if we were running for our lives, but I don't like just stealing the plane because it's here. God can take care of us some other way."

Lionel brought up an e-mail he had received from Sam Goldberg in Israel asking them to come back to Jerusalem. *You won't believe what God is doing here*, Sam wrote.

As they talked and prayed, Judd and Lionel both felt they should still go to Israel. They wanted to see the spectacle Carpathia had planned for the world firsthand.

"Why don't we stay on the plane until it's time to go?" Westin said. "We'll have the whole thing to ourselves, and we won't have to put up with the parties and head-banging music. When Z-Van starts recording, things get wild."

Judd and Lionel brought their things to the plane and settled in. They both had access to the latest computers and communication equipment.

"We should get a conference call together with the rest of the Force," Judd said.

Lionel smiled. "We'll make it a video-conference. That way you can see Vicki."

Late that evening in Iowa, Vicki was sitting up in bed, writing down a few thoughts in her journal when Shelly knocked. She came in, sat on the bed, and asked how Vicki was doing.

Vicki shared her thoughts about Natalie. Then she said, "You didn't tell me what was going on with Cheryl. Is she okay?"

"I don't know how to tell you this and not shock you." Shelly sighed. "Cheryl's going to have a baby."

Vicki's mouth dropped. "Are you sure?"

"We gave her a test and it was positive. She was as shocked as anybody."

"How far along is she?"

"Two, maybe three months."

Vicki thought about Lenore and her baby, Tolan. The child had been such a bright spot in everyone's life at the schoolhouse. But as cute and cuddly as a new baby would be, Vicki knew Cheryl was in for a rough season. "How's she taking the news?"

"She said if she didn't know that God loves

her and forgave her for her sins, she'd probably have an abortion."

"I want to talk with her."

"She's resting now, but there's somebody else who says he needs a word."

"Mark?"

Shelly shook her head. "That cute guy upstairs, Chad. He asked to see if you'd meet with him. He seems really nice."

"Now?" Vicki scowled. "What's he want to talk about?"

"I think he's concerned about you."

Vicki got dressed and started upstairs. She stopped outside the door and listened to the believers gathered in the kitchen. They discussed Carpathia, the guillotines, Tsion Ben-Judah, and the kids downstairs.

"We can't keep them here indefinitely," a man said. "The GC will find out and they'll haul us all in."

"We've already had neighbors snooping around and asking questions," a woman said.

Vicki opened the door a crack and looked at the group. With the exception of Chad, they were all older.

Chad held up a hand. "I know we're all worried about what's going to happen, but let's put ourselves in their place. They came out here and risked their lives to save some brothers and sisters. What if it had been us in that GC compound? You think they would have gotten us out?"

The room fell silent as Chad continued. "Of course they would have. I think the least we can do is help them out as long as we can."

Vicki stepped through the door. Chad introduced her to the rest of the group. "Vicki is the one I told you about who was up on the screen giving kids the gospel in the middle of a Global Community education event."

Several around the room clapped and Vicki smiled. Chad took her hand and pulled her onto the back porch. "I know you've been through something terrible, but I want you to come with me."

"Where? I thought we weren't supposed to go outside."

"Trust me."

Chad grabbed a basket and took Vicki to a dirt bike parked in the garage. Vicki climbed on the back and held the basket while Chad revved the engine and drove into the moonlit night.

He drove over a narrow path that led into a burned-out thicket of trees and bushes. The cool wind felt good and the air was fresh on Vicki's face. Chad seemed to drive like he had traveled the path a thousand times before. He stopped at the edge of the charred trees and pointed to the crest of a hill. Three deer stood at the top, feeding on grass. They glanced toward the motorcycle, then continued eating.

"The plague of fire destroyed a lot of forests and homes around here, but you can still see the beauty God created if you look hard enough."

"I'd almost forgotten how pretty things can be."

Chad leaned the bike against a tree, and the two hiked to the top of the hill. The deer moved across the slope, keeping watch on the two as Chad spread a blanket on the ground. "We got off to a bad start. I didn't mean to upset you when you asked—"

"It's okay. I was stressed." Vicki lifted the lid on the basket but couldn't see inside. "Your friends back at the house don't seem too happy about us being here."

"They're a little worried about their families."

"I can understand that."

"I heard about your friend Cheryl. If there's anything we can do, let me know."

Vicki sighed. "I want her to stay with us, but I don't know how safe she'll be."

"You think she'll keep the baby?"

"I haven't talked with her yet."

Chad glanced away. "I also heard about Natalie. I'm sorry."

Vicki bit her lip and stared at the sky. It had been a long time since she had been outside at night and not on the run. "I can't get her face out of my head. The last time I saw her, I begged her to come with us, but she wouldn't. I feel responsible for her death."

"I don't think she'd feel that way."

"Why not?"

"Let's say you went into that GC compound to help your friends and the GC caught you. Would you blame the others?"

"Of course not. It was my choice to go in there."

"Then why is Natalie any different? She chose to risk her life and she got caught. She wanted to risk it for you and your friends. Don't take that away from her by punishing yourself for her death."

"I hadn't thought about it like that."

"If there's one thing I know, it's that God has a purpose for things. Everything fits together like a puzzle, but we're looking at it from a human angle. All we can see are missing pieces. He sees the big picture and knows how it all fits."

Vicki wiped away a tear. "It doesn't make her death any easier to live with."

"You'd have to be a robot for it not to

hurt." Chad opened the basket and dumped the contents on the blanket. He unwrapped a hot loaf of homemade cinnamon bread and pulled off a piece. "I forgot the knife. This is how they used to do it back in Bible times."

"I'm sure they had cinnamon bread back then." Vicki laughed as she took the bread. It almost melted in her mouth. "So tell me your story."

Chad leaned back on an elbow. "It's pretty boring. My parents were Christians and took my brothers and me to church. I was the oldest and had pretty much decided I was going to have some fun before I got serious about God. I figured I had plenty of time."

"Where were you on the night of the disappearances?"

"I was out late with some guys from my baseball team. We'd have a few beers and drive to Des Moines to see a movie or go to a club that wouldn't kick us out. Our third baseman, Kyle Eastman, never drank with us, but we asked him to come along sometimes because we knew he'd be the only one sober enough to drive home."

"He was a Christian?"

Chad smiled. "We called him the hot-corner preacher. He didn't really preach at us.

We just knew he didn't do the same stuff we did."

"Had you ever prayed before?"

Chad took another piece of bread. "When I was a kid, I'd go to church and listen. Every time the preacher would ask people if they wanted to pray and ask God into their lives, I'd almost do it. Sometimes they'd have you come forward, and a couple of times I almost got up and went, but something held me back. I was embarrassed and didn't want anybody to think I was weak."

"It's not weak to admit you need God."

"I know that now. I wish I could go back and change all that, but the way I look at it, if I had, I wouldn't have met you. Don't blush."

Vicki smiled. "Finish your story."

"Kyle had told his parents where he was going and when he was coming home. When a couple of the guys went off by themselves, he called home and told them he'd be late. It took a couple hours to catch up with our friends, but we finally headed home.

"I was in the front seat next to Kyle, and there were three others in the back, asleep. Kyle started talking to me about spiritual stuff. He asked if I knew where I'd go if I died. I got paranoid and asked if he was going to drive off the road on purpose. He just grinned.

"I told him I believed all the stuff about Jesus, but I wasn't ready to leave my friends and fun yet."

"What did he say?"

"He tried to convince me that I wouldn't be giving up anything if I asked God to forgive me. He said I'd be gaining all of heaven if I just gave God control and let him do what he wanted."

"And?"

"I pretended to pass out. I didn't want to hear it. I knew what he said was true, but I didn't want to face it. As I was sitting there with my head against the seat, I heard Kyle whispering. He was praying for us, asking God to show us the truth and to use him in some way. Then he got quiet. He had the radio tuned to a Christian station and it was on really low.

"That's when the car ran off the road. I looked over and Kyle was gone. There was nothing in the seat except his clothes, his watch, and his baseball jacket."

"Did you wreck?" Vicki said.

"He had the car on cruise control. It drifted off the interstate, and we almost hit a guardrail before I jerked it back onto the road and hit the brake. The guys in back woke up and didn't believe me when I said Kyle had disappeared. They jumped out of the car and looked for him along the road. I knew what had happened and I was scared.

"We were freaking out when another car behind us plowed into the same guardrail we'd almost hit. The car was smashed really bad, and we all ran to see if we could help. The other guys got there first and started screaming. There was nobody inside."

"How long after that was it before you prayed?"

"I didn't waste any time. I prayed right there and told God I was sorry I had waited. I tried to get my friends to pray, but they were scared out of their minds. The Christian radio station Kyle was listening to played a few more songs, and then it went dead. I didn't know whether God would forgive me or if I'd missed my chance. It wasn't until I read a guy's Web site a while later that I knew the truth that God did forgive me and had made me a tribulation saint."

"Did any of your friends pray?"

"Nobody in the car that night. I found some relatives who weren't believers and told them. That's how we all came to the house."

Vicki loved hearing these kinds of stories. She told what had happened to her family and Chad listened closely. When Vicki yawned an hour later, Chad scooted closer.

"I'll get you back to the house, but I need to say something. I know I'm being bold, but the way I see it, we only have about three and a half years before Christ comes back. I'd like to get to know you better."

"I don't know what to say."

"Shelly said you had a boyfriend but that he's away."

"He's not really my boyfriend. We've known each other since the disappearances, but I don't know where our relationship is going."

Chad packed their things in the basket, and they walked down the hill to the dirt bike. Vicki put a hand on his shoulder. "Thanks for talking about Natalie. I feel a lot better."

Chad smiled. "I don't know what you're planning, but I'd be more than glad if you guys want to stay with us."

TWELVE

Crash Landing

JUDD knelt by Lionel in front of the tiny
camera mounted on the computer on
Z-Van's plane. They were only a couple of
days away from Nicolae's appearance in
Israel, and Judd knew from the Bible and
Tsion Ben-Judah's writings that things would
get very bad very quickly. They both smiled
when Darrion appeared on the screen,
wiping her eyes and yawning. Charlie sat in
the background petting Phoenix.

Darrion told them what the kids had been
through. Judd gasped when he heard about
what had happened in Iowa. He put his head
in his hands when Darrion broke the news
about Natalie. Though he had never met the
girl, she had been part of the Young Trib
Force. Darrion told Judd that they hadn't
heard any more about Jim Dekker and Pete
Davidson.

Judd ran a hand through his hair. "Where are Vicki and the others?"

Darrion told him and gave him the number in Iowa. "I know they're trying to get back here, but I think they should stay where they are if they're safe."

Lionel waved at Charlie, and the boy moved to the camera. "I heard you had a pretty close shave with the GC."

Charlie smiled. "Vicki came to get me. But if it wasn't for Natalie, I'd probably be in the head chopper right now."

"Well, we're glad you didn't have to face the head chopper," Lionel said.

Darrion asked where Judd and Lionel were and Judd told her. Darrion shook her head. "At least you guys know how to ride in style."

"We're headed to Israel in the next couple of days with Z-Van and his crew," Judd said. "We're going to join Sam and Mr. Stein, watch the festivities, and try to get back home from there."

"Be careful," Darrion said. "The GC is really cracking down here. When the public starts taking the mark, things will get ugly."

Judd and Lionel prayed with Darrion and Charlie a few minutes, then said good-bye. Judd moved to the back of the plane. He knew it was still early in the Midwest, but he felt like he had to talk to Vicki.

The phone rang twice before Shelly picked up. She seemed thrilled that Judd had called and told him Vicki was still sleeping. "She had a late night with the guy we're staying with. He's really cute."

"She was on a date?" Judd yelled.

"It wasn't like that. Vicki's been torn up about Natalie for days, and Chad took her back on his farm. She told me about it when she came in."

"Fine. I just wanted to make sure you guys were all right and hear your plan."

"We want to get back to Wisconsin, but we don't know when it will be safe. We're trying to decide if we should take some of the people we rescued from the reeducation facility."

"Why would you take them with you?"

"Well, one of them is pregnant and has just become a believer, so we thought she—"

"I don't believe this. . . ."

Shelly paused. "I thought you called because you cared about us. It sounds like you're mad that you can't boss us around."

"Let me talk with Mark."

A few seconds later Mark came to the phone. "What was that all about?"

"I can't believe what's going on back there.

You guys take off halfway across the country and you don't—"

"Whoa, big boy," Mark interrupted. "Take a breath. What's wrong with you?"

"Nothing's wrong with me. I'm upset about the chances you guys are taking."

"If you were here, you'd understand. We got a distress call from Iowa and felt like it was worth the risk."

"And there's at least one believer dead, and maybe more if they catch Pete and this Dekker guy!"

"Judd, calm down. And if you can't, call me back. Do you want us to just sit on our hands until you can help us decide everything? If that's true, we would never have sent The Cube out, and that's been a success beyond our wildest dreams."

Judd took a breath. He looked in one of the many mirrors in Z-Van's plane and saw that his face had reddened. "Can I talk with Vicki?" Judd finally managed.

"If you're going to be like this, I don't think it's a good idea. Natalie's death really hit her hard. She blamed herself for not getting her out of there."

"I just . . . want to talk."

Judd waited, staring at himself in the mirror. He had known Vicki and the others for three and a half years. God had changed him in many ways, helping knock off the rough edges, but he still had a barrelful of anger inside and he had no idea why.

Vicki awoke from a sound sleep with Shelly standing over her. The girl held out the phone. "Judd's on the line for you."

Vicki tried to clear her throat, but her voice still sounded groggy when she said, "Judd, what's up?"

"Darrion told us everything that's happened. I wanted to make sure you're all right."

Judd sounded tense. Vicki scrunched her eyes and sat up. "Things could be better, but we're relatively safe. Just waiting to get back to Wisconsin."

"I should have gotten in touch with you a long time ago. So much has been going on over here."

"Any news on when you're coming back?"

Judd told her about their planned trip to Israel. "We want to see Sam and Mr. Stein again and watch Carpathia's next show-down." Judd paused. "Vick, about this Chad guy . . ."

"What about him?"

Another pause. "I don't know. I guess . . ."

"What?" Vicki said warily.

"I think Z-Van and his crew are headed to the plane. I need to go."

"Okay, be careful."

"I will. Good-bye."

Vicki clicked the off button, and Shelly came back in the room. The two shared notes about his call, and Shelly said she thought Judd was way out of line.

When Vicki told her that Judd had mentioned Chad, Shelly threw up her hands. "I thought you'd appreciate me stirring up the competitive juices."

Vicki frowned. "I don't need anybody competing over me. We don't have time for those games." She lay back and put an arm over her forehead. "Do you remember anyone named Ben or Brad?"

Shelly shook her head. "Why?"

"I went to sleep thinking about Cheryl and her baby. Part of me thinks she should place the child with someone older who will know how to care for it."

"Like Lenore?" Shelly said.

"Lenore would be perfect. But when I woke up, those two names came to me and I can't figure out why."

Shelly whistled. "Maybe I can make Judd jealous of them too."

"Maybe it was too much cinnamon bread

last night, but I can't help thinking it means something."

Judd and Lionel retreated to the back of the plane as Westin raced through warning that Z-Van was near. "You guys stay out of sight and they'll probably never notice you."

Judd peeked into the main cabin after they were airborne and noticed that Z-Van's manager and his band members now had the mark of Carpathia. They joked and toasted each other.

Z-Van pulled out a piece of paper and asked for quiet. "His Excellency gave me this before we left. He even has a melody picked out for it."

"He wrote this himself?" one of the band members said.

"Here's how it goes." Z-Van lifted his head and closed his eyes, as if he were uttering something sacred.

> *Hail Carpathia, our lord and risen king;*
> *Hail Carpathia, rules o'er everything.*
> *We'll worship him until we die;*
> *He's our beloved Nicolae.*
> *Hail Carpathia, our lord and risen king.*

People in the room clapped and asked Z-Van to sing it again. Soon they all joined in with an off-key version of the hymn to the Antichrist.

Lionel shook his head. "I think we made a big mistake coming with these people."

Two days later, Vicki and the others joined in the basement hideout as Mark called the kids together. He stood at the computer with an e-mail message opened. "This came on the Web site early this morning."

> *Dear Young Tribulation Force,*
> *I need your help. My name is Claudia Zander. I was Natalie Bishop's roommate. Before she died, she talked with me about God. I didn't want to listen at first, but now that she's gone, I think what she said might be true. She told me not to take the mark of Carpathia, and I've only got a few more days to comply.*
> *Please write back.*
> *Claudia*

Mark looked at Vicki. "Did Natalie really have a roommate?"

Vicki nodded. "Natalie said she was a rabid follower of Carpathia."

"Then it must be a trick," Conrad said.

Vicki pursed her lips. "What if it isn't? Can we afford to not try and help her?"

Judd and Lionel walked the streets of Tel Aviv, where the GC planned to open the first loyalty mark application site to the public. It was a festive atmosphere, almost like a carnival, as people gawked at the sub-potentates' vehicles on their way to meet with Carpathia.

Judd couldn't wait to get to Jerusalem to see Sam and Mr. Stein, but Westin had convinced them to stay until the whole group went there. "You don't want to miss Z-Van's debut of his new songs, right?"

Judd had rolled his eyes. The thought of more songs devoted to praising Carpathia turned his stomach. What he really wanted to see was the man who would stand up to Carpathia, as foretold in Scripture. Though Judd didn't know for sure, he suspected it would be Tsion Ben-Judah, and he wondered if the man might spare a few moments with him.

The streets were packed with people from all over the world waiting to see the risen potentate in person. People spoke in different languages and were animated about what would happen in Jerusalem. Some said Carpathia would destroy the Judah-ites the same way he had the two prophets, Eli and Moishe. Others said there were massive protests planned by Judah-ites and Orthodox Jews and that a special weapon was being shipped to Jerusalem to annihilate anyone who came against the Global Community's chosen one.

"Why do they need a weapon when they have god himself," one woman said, "and his right-hand man, the Most High Reverend Fortunato?"

Streets clogged with cars and pedestrians. Judd and Lionel followed the crowds to the seashore, where an amphitheater had been quickly constructed. One area was overrun with people standing in line, and Judd went for a closer look. He wasn't surprised to find it was the site where citizens would take Carpathia's mark.

Judd and Lionel skirted the masses and stood on the shore where they could see the stage and not be hemmed in by the crowds. A few minutes later, a caravan of cars pulled up and the most powerful people in the world walked onto the platform. The crowd went wild.

Nicolae Carpathia thanked everyone for welcoming them so warmly. He talked about the improvements in the world since the Global Community had come into existence and said that he felt a renewed energy for the task ahead.

The crowd laughed when Nicolae attributed his vigor to the "three days of the best sleep I've ever had." They cheered again when the potentate said there would be a special musical presentation by the most popular entertainer in the world.

First, he introduced Leon Fortunato, head of all Carpathia worship. Leon knelt and kissed Nicolae's hand, then moved to the podium. "Allow me to teach you a new anthem that focuses on the one who died for us and now lives for us."

"Uh-oh, here it comes." Lionel sighed.

The crowd quickly picked up the lyrics to "Hail Carpathia, Our Lord and Risen King" and sang along. Judd turned when he noticed a loud droning and saw a sleek aircraft heading over the city toward the site.

"As you can tell," Carpathia said, taking the podium again, "we have another surprise for you. The plane you see in the distance carries not only the equipment needed for this site, but also a brief display of its capabilities, ably demonstrated by the pilot of my own Phoenix 216, Captain Mac McCullum. Enjoy."

With that, Carpathia stepped back and was surrounded by the other sub-potentates at the back of the stage. The jet screamed over the crowd, very low and fast, and surged toward the Mediterranean Sea.

"I guess Mac is still employed by the GC," Lionel whispered. "Wonder when he'll leave?"

The plane flew so low it looked like it skimmed the water, then turned and flew over the stage. Judd noticed that a few of the sub-potentates wanted to duck, but they kept their places, squinting to see the plane speed past.

The plane eventually flew out over the water and shot straight up. When it reached the peak of its climb, it seemed to stop in midair and drift toward the ground.

"Something's not right," Lionel said.

The nose of the plane turned and plunged toward the water at a frightening speed. People around Judd laughed and pointed, thinking this was part of the show. "Pull out, pull out," Judd whispered as the plane rocketed toward earth.

But it did not pull out. The plane, a technological marvel of the Global Community, slammed into the beach at hundreds of miles an hour. The shock of seeing the sure death of Mac McCullum and his crew, along with the explosion of the aircraft itself, sent Judd to his knees.

"Please, God, not another death among the Tribulation Force."

ABOUT THE AUTHORS

Jerry B. Jenkins (www.jerryjenkins.com) is the writer of the Left Behind series. He owns the Jerry B. Jenkins Christian Writers Guild, an organization dedicated to mentoring aspiring authors. Former vice president for publishing for the Moody Bible Institute of Chicago, he also served many years as editor of *Moody* magazine and is now Moody's writer-at-large.

His writing has appeared in publications as varied as *Reader's Digest, Parade, Guideposts,* in-flight magazines, and dozens of other periodicals. Jenkins's biographies include books with Billy Graham, Hank Aaron, Bill Gaither, Luis Palau, Walter Payton, Orel Hershiser, and Nolan Ryan, among many others. His books appear regularly on the *New York Times, USA Today, Wall Street Journal,* and *Publishers Weekly* bestseller lists.

Jerry is also the writer of the nationally syndicated sports story comic strip *Gil Thorp,* distributed to newspapers across the United States by Tribune Media Services.

Jerry and his wife, Dianna, live in Colorado and have three grown sons.

Dr. Tim LaHaye (www.timlahaye.com), who conceived the idea of fictionalizing an account of the Rapture and the Tribulation, is a noted author, minister, and nationally recognized speaker on Bible prophecy. He is the founder of both Tim LaHaye Ministries and The PreTrib Research Center. He also recently cofounded the Tim LaHaye School of Prophecy at Liberty University. Presently Dr. LaHaye speaks at many of the major Bible prophecy conferences in the U.S. and Canada, where his current prophecy books are very popular.

Dr. LaHaye holds a doctor of ministry degree from Western Theological Seminary and a doctor of literature degree from Liberty University. For twenty-five years he pastored one of the nation's outstanding churches in San Diego, which grew to three locations. It was during that time that he founded two accredited Christian high schools, a Christian school system of ten schools, and Christian Heritage College.

Dr. LaHaye has written over forty books that have been published in more than thirty languages. He has written books on a wide variety of subjects, such as family life, temperaments, and Bible prophecy. His current fiction works, the Left Behind series, written with Jerry B. Jenkins, continue to appear on the best-seller lists of the Christian Booksellers Association, *Publishers Weekly, Wall Street Journal, USA Today*, and the *New York Times*.

He is the father of four grown children and grandfather of nine. Snow skiing, waterskiing, motorcycling, golfing, vacationing with family, and jogging are among his leisure activities.

The Future Is Clear

Check out the exciting Left Behind: The Kids series

Books #31 and #32 coming soon!

Hooked on the exciting
Left Behind: The Kids series?
Then you'll love the dramatic audios!

Listen as the characters come to life in this theatrical
audio that makes the saga of those left behind
even more exciting.

High-tech sound effects, original music,
and professional actors will have you
on the edge of your seat.

Experience the heart-stopping action and
suspense of the end times for yourself!

Three exciting volumes available on CD or cassette.